The GERANIUM WINDOW

Beatrice MacNeil

P.O. Box 2188, St. John's, NL, Canada, A1C 6E6
WWW.BREAKWATERBOOKS.COM

LIBRARY AND ARCHIVES CANADA CATALOGUING IN PUBLICATION
MacNeil, Beatrice, 1945-, author
The geranium window / Beatrice MacNeil.
ISBN 978-1-55081-661-7 (paperback)
I. Title.
PS8575.N43G47 2016   C813'.54   C2016-905775-5

 Canada Council
for the Arts   Conseil des Arts
du Canada   Canada   Newfoundland
Labrador

We acknowledge the support of the Canada Council for the Arts, which last year
invested $153 million to bring the arts to Canadians throughout the country.
We acknowledge the Government of Canada through the Canada Book Fund
and the Government of Newfoundland and Labrador through the Department
of Tourism, Culture and Recreation for our publishing activities.

PRINTED AND BOUND IN CANADA.

Breakwater Books is committed to choosing papers and materials for our
books that help to protect our environment. To this end, this book is printed
on a recycled paper that is certified by the Forest Stewardship Council®.

RECYCLED
Paper made from
recycled material
FSC® C103567

IN LOVING MEMORY

of my cherished friend and neighbour, Clark,

and the summer days and winter nights

spent on the Lake Road in Lower L'Ardoise,

Cape Breton.

part
ONE

1

THE FIRST TIME he saw him, the boy was naked. It was a Sunday. The small room Alfie Johns looked into was stark but clean, stripped of all the necessities a young boy banks on for memories: a poster or two, his first poem, a baseball bat, a pair of dirty socks, a hockey-card collection, an assortment of comic books.

The wooden walls were in identical scale to the floor, a pale green hue like new grass. A row of nails along the back wall supported a sparse wardrobe: a pair of pants, a blue plaid shirt, a sweater with arm patches, a pair of pant braces, a worn brown belt coiled up like a cinnamon roll. No dress-up wear. No shiny shoes. A chipped white chamber pail, with a red rim along the cover, sat in the corner of the room. The smell of disinfectant fermented the air.

In the middle of the floor, Joseph Briar cupped in his closed fists the rhythm he was pounding on a makeshift drum, a hollowed-out tree stump with an animal hide tied around its circumference by a rope. He was elf-like in size for a boy of twelve, with a short stubby nose spreading across his pale face. His dark hair was cropped close to his head with several dents running in crooked lines, caused no doubt by the razor's teeth biting into his skull when he had protested. A permanent droop to his bottom lip the appearance of a fat worm folded in two. The slimness of his body forced his ribs to protrude. He reminded Alfie of a character from a children's book.

He remained sightless to his surroundings, his eyes closed while he pounded on his drum, a stream of pure, uncensored sexual rhapsody. Beneath the cave in his chest, the small drum snuggled close like another heart. The drum song sparked a fire in his slight bones. His streaked head swayed from side to side. A wounded butterfly about to land. There was no way of knowing if Joseph had names for the sounds he produced. Perhaps words were unnecessary; the birds outside his window sang without a syllable.

Like the Greek god Pan, the bearer of the mystical, he sits in his twisted limbs waiting for noises. The mystery of his condition in itself may have caused this unfinished child of God to not grow any bigger. He appeared much wiser than the schoolboys who came to stare in stunned curiosity at him, by invitation of his older brother, Arthur, who charged a quarter for a glimpse through the window.

Joseph watched for birds he never knew by name,

but they did not watch for him. They sang their songs, then flew away. He never went outdoors. Few people even knew the Briars had this third child.

Fourteen-year-old Alfie, a school mate of Joseph's older siblings, Anntell and Arthur, appeared at his window without invitation, with music coming from between his teeth. He was alone, and when he smiled down at Joseph, there was left-over music still on his mouth.

"Hello," he said to Joseph. "I heard the beat of your drum."

Joseph listened in silence. He was not accustomed to window voices that spoke directly to him. The others who came just laughed or stared. Perhaps out of fear at what a quarter could produce, or under threat from Arthur Briar that they keep their mouths shut or he would deal with them.

Joseph Briar, born of original shame, the product of an old sperm and a soft egg; his stern, sixty-one-year-old father laid down the fundamental lie. He and Rosie, his much younger wife, had two children only— Anntell and Arthur. This hard rule, this telling deceit, set down by Duncan Briar, was not to be taken lightly. There was no room in the life of a man of his position for any grotesque accident between the sheets. He cursed himself for not having taken the necessary precautions sooner. Instead, shortly after, he had himself severed and tied in a New York hospital. He explained to his wife angrily, "I had no choice. I can't trust the delicacies of a woman's body not to leak out another child." But Duncan Briar did not anticipate the cost of that first lie, the cost his family would pay for that deception.

Alfie Johns knew something about abandonment. He had found, by accident, a letter in the Bible of Bertha Johns, the woman who reared him as her son. It had been written by his birth mother. Childless, Bertha and Wilfred Johns had agreed to take him for a year and possible adoption, if she, the mother, would have no contact with the child.

The weight in Alfie's shoulders spread throughout his body. He felt much older than his years as he stood in the grey day surrounded by the green snarled arms of the trees. He knew instinctively the feeling of separation, but the separation Joseph Briar was living came from within his own walls. Alfie understood the rules here: this was it for Joseph Briar. But as he watched the fragile boy pull himself up to the window ledge, he sensed something had changed in both their worlds.

Alfie knew he had to see Joseph again. The desire became a yearning for a dangerous mission; the dare of having a classmate sneak you the answers to an unexpected test, the image of the teacher's pleated, white hands pulling your paper from your desk, and your zero rolling out into your palm. But this one was different. Arthur Briar, full of sermon and one quarter down, could be right around the corner.

And only last week, as Alfie had his hands tucked securely between his legs and his ecstasy mapped out in his head, his adopted mother had come into his room and reminded him to say his prayers before he got too tired. He smiled as the image of Anntell Briar's face slid deeper under his cotton sheet. He had another reason to be interested in the Briar family, now that he knew this young boy was real.

The air was laden with moisture on his second visit to Joseph Briar, a forerunner of the heavy rain forecast for the late-spring morning. Alfie turned up his collar before he took another step towards the big house engulfed in freshly wounded limbs. Joseph's room was situated at the far corner of the grey three-storey house standing well back, almost hidden, from the road. It appeared to have been added on at a distance from the rest.

He knew the Briars were in church on Sunday mornings; clumsy Arthur, no doubt, throwing a quarter from his commerce reluctantly into the collection plate. He smiled when he heard the thumping sounds that floated out from the open window with its faded, rolled-up blind. The row of geranium plants in tin cans on the ledge resembled a line of fat soldiers waiting for inspection.

Alfie watched the boy as his hands rested on the floor. Beside him, rolled up in a ball, were a pair of cotton shorts and a striped short-sleeved sweater he had removed. He lifted his head slowly and looked towards the sound outside his window. Alfie ran his mouth organ along his sleeve and stuffed it back into his shirt pocket as Joseph's twisted body unfolded slowly in a spastic gesture of painful grace. Joseph pushed himself up by his elbows and stood awkwardly in the middle of the room. He swayed on his turned-out feet for balance. He took one step on his bird-like legs, his thin arms held up in the manner of an infant who wanted to be held.

Alfie stood in deep silence. A murder of crows in the distance cawed loudly to one another. He watched the excitement fill up in the round dark eyes of the boy's pasty face. Joseph took a few more steps toward the window with his arms still outstretched. His testicles hung like a child's crude clay model about to crumble. Alfie watched him approach with a crooked grin on his face, smeared with a tinge of pain. It hurt Joseph Briar to smile.

Alfie knew they would not be disturbed by Joseph's blind grandmother, sitting in her rocking chair by the kitchen hearth. Joseph's hands gripped the window ledge as he looked up at Alfie Johns in front of him. His face traceable as a map.

One of Alfie's neighbours always arrived with a story of the war or the womb to leave in Bertha Johns' ear.

He recalled her, now, whispering about Joseph Briar's forty-year-old mother, too weak with pain to cry out, only whimpering the morning Joseph was born. Isla Jones felt the swell of her daughter at her feet and knew instinctively what her blind hands would have to do. The womb cast Joseph Briar out into the world two months too early, like someone who had defaulted on his rent.

Rosie Briar was hard on death. She defied it and her child lived. She wrapped Joseph in cotton batting and placed him on the oven door in a shoebox from Eaton's. No doctor was ever called. Joseph lived in an oven womb for months. Joseph's father was out in the field with Arthur and Anntell when his second son arrived. He didn't expect the child to live beyond the day. Perhaps that's what the sixty-one-year-old Duncan Briar wished for his youngest son: death in a shoebox. The child would be an embarrassment if it lived; the village would look down on Duncan, would mock him for having an erection at his age, and its result amounting to nothing more than this bird-like specimen. So he kept Joseph hidden, and forbade his wife and mother-in-law to reveal his existence.

Alfie Johns heard a different story about the child leaking out to schoolboys in recess circles. In hushed tones, Arthur told about the circus boy his mother had rescued from the mainland in Nova Scotia. How she brazenly opened the tent and retrieved the freak boy, whom she felt was mistreated, while his caretakers were swallowing fire on the main stage. She wrapped him in a sweater and took him home. Arthur never mentioned the role Joseph played in the circus, but he began to let them see the freak for themselves, to take reservations. Only four at a time were allowed to see the boy.

Curiosity is more powerful than any secret. Duncan Briar was wrong to believe his other son would be frightened into silence. Locked in that dangerous space between being clumsy and being unloved, Arthur Briar craved attention. His path of destruction left footprints early. Arthur was not sure if his brother Joseph even recognized his name. He tried to get him to repeat it. "Arthur, my name is Arthur. I know you have it hidden away somewhere, Joseph. Can you say Ar...thur?" He wanted to hear the sound of Joseph's voice. Joseph looked up at him. His eyes soulful as his small hand touched Arthur's mouth in search of the word.

They came together on Sunday mornings at his father's insistence—his mother, his sister, and himself—for their souls' weekly maintenance. The blind and the breakable were beyond repair, and so beyond salvation, according to Duncan Briar. They remained behind closed doors as the others piled into Duncan's shiny Ford Coupe. Isla, Rosie's mother, kept her ear to any unusual sounds from Joseph's room. This was the day of the week that Arthur hated his father most, his commands and his fucking rules. He knew his father went to see, and hear about, his generous donations to the church. And since Arthur refused to pray for anything (he was positive that none of his family did either), he always referred to Sunday as the "Coupe Loop."

Anntell Briar walked on ahead of the others as if she had been redirected by a slice of wind. She preferred her own space. She resisted conversation with anyone. She blocked out all sermons. She was reading *The Scarlet Letter* by Nathaniel Hawthorne and was quite taken by the advantages that might be available to her beautiful mother had she had the courage of Hester Prynne. There was something about adultery that intrigued Anntell. She would never marry an older man as her mother had, whatever the circumstances. Old men dulled the best part of fiction, she boasted to a bewildered English teacher one afternoon, in a contemptuous rapture of adolescent knowledge.

Rosie Briar walked with a slight limp, her leg twisted by childhood polio. At fifty-one, she wore her brace for safety's sake. Sometimes, she even forgot about it; it followed behind her like a harmless stalker, an invisible displeasure, until she looked down.

Duncan Briar, cruel and haunted, moved slowly through the crowd of people gathered at the front of the church. He was a heavy-set man who made his money early in life, and kept it to his advantage. He owned the Briar Mill, but paid someone else to run it. At seventy-one years of age, the retired shipbuilder was still in touch with the local, national, and worldly politics of the day. He was well educated and proud, and kept his dialogue to a few sentences around his peers. When he was thirty-seven, Duncan Briar had hired the beautiful young Rosie Jones to care for his ailing mother's personal needs, and married her shortly after his mother's death. Being twenty years older than his wife, he didn't carry what he considered the knots of a long marriage like an old ship. His wife still looked fresh to him, his anchor he could cast at any time.

Arthur watched his mother climb the church steps between the peals of the bell on Sunday mornings. A slow delight of the muscles in her soft legs resembled a dancer's. He watched them ripple, lap against each delicate bone in her smooth flesh. Each step deliberate and defiant as her feet touched the wooden steps. She turned and took Arthur by the arm as he escorted her to the front pew. She had not come here for a miracle. It had already arrived for her, and the only peal that held her attention at the moment came from the beat of a small drum she longed to get back home to hear.

Alfie Johns checked his watch. The Briars would be home in another ten minutes or so. Joseph watched his every movement and had settled himself on the floor in front of the window in a sitting position now. Alfie spoke softly to him.

"My name is Alfie."

Joseph grinned up at him.

"Would you like me to play another tune for you?"

The boy lifted his right hand as if he were about to ask a question. Alfie played a lively jig as he watched the child's face light up. His hands trembled in the air, a delicate image of a dying bird in a wooden cage.

"Did you like that tune, Joseph?" Alfie held up his mouth organ for the child to see, and ran it against his mouth to show him where the music came from.

Joseph folded his small hands over and over, as if shuffling a deck of cards. He must have been half the weight of an average twelve year old. His skin, a pale river blue despite the heat of the day; he resembled an exotic bird that had emerged from cool water and nestled in a deep clearing. It was obvious he loved company.

Alfie studied the boy's face and wondered what had kept him alive for a dozen years. He hated the appellation "slow" applied to any human being. Slow to what? Die? The boy was happy with his own sounds. He had the gifts of touch and of sight and of hearing; he was able to move his muscles painfully into what everyone else in his family sought, the illusions or delusions of happiness.

"You do understand me, don't you, Joseph?" Alfie's words were drowned in the dark pools of Joseph's eyes.

"I will come back to visit you. We can watch the birds."

The child stared up at him, a knowing look on his face.

I know, said his eyes, *I know*.

Alfie touched Joseph lightly on the head as he pulled himself up to the window ledge. He felt sure the boy was loved dearly by his mother, and that whatever condition he had could afflict anyone's child. It had to be Duncan Briar's idea to keep the child out of sight. He had seen the man in the village, an imposing breath of anger seething between his lips when he spoke.

A heavy rain fell as Alfie made his way home. He clutched his hand firmly shut into an angry fist as he stumbled into the dents in the road the rain created.

2

THE FACE OF the hidden child of Rocky Point kept Alfie restless. What had he really expected to see on that first Sunday visit? Certainly not a real child concealed in wood. Arthur may have constructed a dummy hidden behind a mask, he thought, and had a great laugh at the expense of others. It was something Arthur was capable of doing for a laugh. That was what he had expected to see when he decided to check the place out when the Briars went to church.

Alfie wanted to preserve everything about Joseph Briar, now that he knew a real child existed within the Briar walls. He took his camera on his second visit the following Sunday. He wanted to keep Joseph close to him, at his drum, squatting on the planks. His pain-smeared smile. His broken steps as he approached the geraniums and the stranger with the music and the strange object in his hand that stole the images that would break Alfie's heart.

He wondered if Joseph was at peace while he slept

beside his silent drum. He closed his eyes on this image before drifting off into a disturbed sleep. In Alfie's dream, Joseph killed off the geraniums, one leaf left leaning against the window. Their red petals bled along the window's edge, splattered on Joseph as he played in their small pool at his feet. Joseph spoke to him in the voice of a much older person.

"Everything that lives must die its own death: flowers, words, even music when it breaths its last notes."

His thin voice seemed to float from underwater. Joseph was fearless. His eyes looked calm; he had been relieved of the baggage of unspoken words. His muscles appeared much firmer, stronger. His hair, full of dark curls, reached his shoulders. He was fully dressed with his little cinnamon-bun belt tucked securely in place. He appeared as peaceful as a Hermetic monk.

Alfie awoke at five a.m. to the tick-tick of his alarm clock in his left ear and an ache in the middle of his forehead. The morning was still in silhouette. It had stopped raining. He lay back under his sheet and wondered if Joseph Briar ever had dreams. How did he settle them down? Or did his mother know that her child stirred in her own uneven sleep? Alfie wondered if Joseph would remember him the next time he appeared at his window to play him a tune.

He would have to approach the house carefully to make sure Arthur didn't see him. There was a wounded, uneven streak in Arthur Briar. He spoke with a stammer when he was agitated or stressed. Something about this infirmity amused him; it got people's attention. His "fuck-off" lasted as long as the spell he claimed he could put on anyone. He had a clever mind but it could be easily distracted from logic. He was the tallest in the class, over six-feet tall in grade nine, another advantage he had when his temper exploded.

Alfie asked him once, in a casual, friendly manner, about the boy he heard him mention to some of the kids.

"That's none of your business, Johns. Go to hell with your fucking questions!"

"I'll bet your father doesn't know what you told them, Arthur; all those stories about the circus."

"The old man couldn't give a damn about…" Arthur left the rest of his sentence in mid-air; he was nervous around him. Alfie always wanted an answer to every question, thought Arthur, was always sizing up the conversation at hand. A real mole digger. He knew the right questions to ask, and Arthur would have to come up with the wrong answers in a hurry.

"What about Anntell, did you tell her?"

"She's like the old man; she doesn't talk to anyone. I can't stand that ugly bookworm face of hers. Why? You got the hots for her, Alfie? She doesn't give a damn for anything. The bitch will get the old man's loot. Is that why you're so damn interested?"

Arthur gave Alfie a poisonous stare. He hated being

cornered like a rat. But he was careful. Alfie Johns was almost his size. He was smart and he knew something about him that the wind could carry a disastrous distance. He knew also that if Alfie spoke to his father, his little commercial venture would be over. He'd be out of the house at the end his old man's fist. What would his mother think of him if she knew? He would never want to hurt her. The scene in Arthur's head went round and round, spinning out of control. What did Alfie capture with that camera of his that he carried around strapped to his shoulder? Arthur wondered. The old bastard would be livid if he knew that Alfie Johns had figured out what was really going on in the Briar household. He turned his glare again on Alfie.

"You heard fuck-all, Alfie. I tell those morons what they want to hear. Laughing is their best subject at school. They couldn't divide a deck of cards between them. If you want something to be believed, tell the stupid first. You, always hanging around like a calf on an udder, looking for something to snap at. Why don't you f-off with that camera of yours!"

"Did you show those morons what they wanted to see?"

Alfie knew he had pushed him too far. He was not only angry; Arthur Briar was afraid. Anger and fear are an insult to the ego. Alfie would have to diffuse the situation.

"I saw your mother in the store on Saturday; she is a

nice lady."

Arthur's face was pliable. He looked more like a ten year old as he stood eye to eye with Alfie.

"So?"

"So, you're lucky to have such a nice mother."

"She's nicer than the old man. He's a pig."

Alfie ignored this confession. He grinned at Arthur pretending not to have heard his last remark. His voice mellowed. Something had hit a nerve.

"She is very pretty, too. Your sister Anntell looks like her. They have the same features."

"Anntell looks like a worm. She belongs at the end of a hook."

"Your mother is pretty."

Arthur's eyes softened.

"She dances sometimes when she thinks nobody's looking. She turns on the radio in the front room and closes the drapes. She moves around in her bare feet, dancing slowly. Reminds me of a dancer in a shadow box. I watch her from the kitchen in case she falls. My grandmother can't see any of this. She's blind, you know, has been for years. Her eyes are the colour of a silver fox. The old man's mother died before I was born. He says I have his mother's poison eyes. I don't know what the hell happened to his old man. He never mentions him."

Arthur Briar's eyes turned a savage blue when he mentioned his father.

"I've never seen your grandmother, Arthur. Your mother's mother."

"And you never will as long as the old man is still breathing. He doesn't even speak to her. He tells me to take her to bed first thing every night. Sometimes it's not even dark, and I know she is aware that there is still light all around her, but she never complains. She just moves quietly down the hall on my arm."

"That's too bad."

"Why in the hell are you so interested in the old fool?"

"I'm not. I asked you about what I heard you tell the group of kids."

"I made it all up. Some people will believe anything. I've never been to a circus. My old man said I don't need the company of fools. I just have to look in a mirror."

Perhaps he was ashamed that he had leaked the details of the divided Briar family, the hatred and love stored between those walls. His mother's desire to dance behind the silver eyes of her own mother, and how he led his grandmother down a dark hall with the light of day all around her. And little Joseph, in his own shade of the house. How much did he really look at him in all these years? Had Joseph ever seen his mother dance? Arthur Briar could not reveal this information without revealing his own downfall. He shared few words with Anntell who danced up a storm in her room. She didn't mind if anyone saw her. "I was born to be seen," she boasted.

It is difficult to hold a love-hate conversation with someone, even yourself. Every syllable is twisted in your mouth, tugging at a moral bridle with nobody pulling the reins. He was skeptical of Alfie Johns and his clear voice asking the right questions. Why was he so interested in his family, the Briars?

Arthur turned, without another word, and shuffled off with the gait of a weary old man, out of the conversation and towards the school. His lanky frame disappeared out of sight behind the school, a trail of boys of uneven heights behind him with their hands in their pockets, circling their quarters.

3

THE DAY ALFIE Johns found the letter tucked between the Book of Genesis and the Book of Exodus, he was looking for a photo of an eagle he'd taken down at the Salmon River and placed between the book's pages to keep its edges from curling up.

The letter, in elegant penmanship, was written, from what Alfie could understand, by his biological mother, witnessed by Bertha's aunt, a case worker, and signed by Bertha and her husband Wilfred. The case worker had initiated the turnover because she felt the girl, identified only as Clare, was incapable of raising a hen, although she put up one heck of a battle to keep the poor child. This information was penned in a separate letter from the case worker, and postmarked Louis-bourg 1949, before Alfie was given to Bertha and Wilfred Johns.

The Bible and its secrets lived for years on the long oak table in the hallway entrance. The table was covered with a white runner, like an altar. It was visible to all who knocked on their front door to collect something or to ask directions to the Salmon River. Bertha invited people in and gave them the rundown on the Bible, how it had been in her family for years and as visible as the cowlicks they inherited.

Bertha Johns congratulated herself on her kindness with food. She was proud to be seen with her platters, piled high to entice the palate. She took pleasure in knowing she had stuffed down the throats of the bereaved and the hysterical something sweet or nourishing that might settle their nerves for a time. But there is a difference between being generous and borrowing the traits of piety, bending to her bare knees to fetch her own rewards from her oven. She was a big, homely, reddish-haired woman, who loved wakes and funerals. She'd be the first to offer a plate of something to the mourners, winter or summer. She needed to be needed at summer festivals and weddings, but death added extra spice to her cooking, her favourite recipe was rabbit stew. She inquired daily about the sick; her oven was always on the ready.

Wilfred Johns was a crude-spoken fisherman who often discussed domestic and personal matters with his wife while her head was stuck in the oven checking something. She answered him as if from a cave.

"Not this minute, I'm not in the mood." When she emerged, red as a boiled lobster, she'd run outdoors and sit in the shade with a jar of Noxzema. She refused to be seen as a burnt-out cook.

Alfie quickly surmised that he had been handed into the arms of Bertha Johns like an apple pie, one whose apples had been seeded in recklessness and irresponsible behaviour. The word "love" had been edited from this family. They bought him gifts when they were required and fed him well physically, all the things good parents did for their children. But they took no pride in his gifted mind, mainly because they were unaware that the child was much sharper than they. In fact, they thought it strange a child his age had such bizarre and unusual interests in cameras and drawing.

At six years of age, Alfie realized he looked nothing like them, or any of his so-called cousins, with their splatter of freckles and orange cowlicks. Alfie Johns had deep-set blue eyes and a mass of blond curls he refused to untangle with a comb. By the age of ten, he was rarely taken on fishing excursions by his adopted father. Wilfred said Alfie preferred to take bloody pictures of the fish, rather than catch or clean them. A camera was not an asset on the high seas. These toys of his were an attribute of his reckless origins, a legacy they could do without in their home.

They refused to pose for him. Images of them, taken by a slow, illegitimate child, were out of the question. Once he asked them to pose on the broken limb of an apple tree behind a basket of freshly picked apples

Bertha had rescued from a storm. They were outraged that Alfie wanted to turn them into some post-war Adam and Eve. But he had outdone them and caught them off-guard: Bertha with her head in the oven was a gem, Wilfred's hand grabbing at her derriere as if she were on fire.

Alfie took a job at the local grocery store on weekends and after school, restocking the shelves to earn money for a new camera—a Hasselblad, the Cadillac of cameras. He saved every penny. He collected bottles and cut grass. He shovelled snow and mended fences and piled wood into sheds for coming winters. He painted barns and tore down old fences.

His deep love for photography grew out of the pages of a *National Geographic* magazine he found in the school library. He sneaked it home in his schoolbag, hid it under his mattress, and slept on its rainbow of colours. Within a couple of months, he had subscribed and was receiving his own magazines. Once, in a picture of an old farmer in Peru, he had seen the beginning of a boil in the folds of the farmer's dark skin. It rose like the crest of a full moon between two clouds. These were the kind of photos that Alfie Johns envisioned in his future.

The power of a zoom lens lived in his head. He imagined it a soft bullet that could hit the skin without penetration. It could capture a falling tear as it descended, a flower birthing from the womb of nature, the sun escaping from a dark cloud, the smile of a nun in deep prayer, a child's delight at the unexpected appearance of a leaping frog. He dreamt of that perfect emotion that practice could not imitate. He studied photographic magazines; he studied lighting and settings, and depth of field and the art of framing a great shot. The determination to learn the mechanics of the camera trembled within him.

4

ANNTELL BRIAR WAS a beauty. Her long, black hair exploded down her back when she emerged from a swim in the Salmon River, her flesh of shimmering glass. Slippery and dangerous, just the way she liked it. When she emerged on the mat of the river's moss, she lay full out and rested in the sun with her long arms outstretched and her hands held loose as if she expected something to fall into them.

Alfie watched this slippery beauty from behind a maple tree. He had six or seven frames left on his roll of film. He couldn't move in too close when the river was quiet, fearing she would hear the click from the shutter, and thunder off like a wild mare. It's not that Anntell Briar objected to being photographed. But she would make her own rules, and want to pose her limbs to their best advantage.

"I don't take X-rays, Anntell," he said laughingly. Alfie preferred real life photos, the kind that caught people in the spaces between moments of superficial decorum.

He stayed quiet as he looked down at her body. He climbed up two or three branches for a better angle. She bent one leg and stretched it full length in the air. Her skin was darker than her brother's, a bronzed risk of flesh that defied danger in her red two-piece bathing suit. The white soles of her feet faced the river like soft beginnings of rare moss. Her bare midriff collected the sun's rays in a melted butter drip. She ran her hand along its smooth lines as if she were spreading it out. He sneaked down and crawled along the bank, as near as he could get without being noticed. A gaggle of geese sang over the river. Alfie smiled as he focused his lens on her sculptured feet nestled amid the grass. Click. Click.

She looked much older than her fifteen years. Her mouth bloomed in a soft curve, but produced hard sentences. Anntell sat two desks ahead of Alfie in school. She was feisty and satisfied by her own intelligence. Her scribblers were adorned with gold stars and black messages. The best reader in the class, she lived in a fictional world of novels. The other girls stayed away from her in clusters, like troops mounting a mutiny. They were not afraid of her, but of their own femininity. They looked young and naïve enough to stroll along the roads with rag dolls in their old prams. They wore ribbons in their hair to match their dresses. They were still reading *Anne of Green Gables* and the *Bobbsey Twins*. It's not that they hadn't gathered in private and discussed sex, but they took the pledge amongst themselves at recess in a hopscotch square to refrain from any of this go-ahead that Anntell advertised as human nature, as libido. They would preserve themselves like their grandmother's fruitcakes—wrapped and sealed for years to enhance the flavour. And God help anyone who broke the seal before due time.

The teacher had been called out by the principal on an urgent matter. Anntell Briar loved urgent-matter times. She had a free platform for her views. She held up *Anna Karenina* in the classroom: "This is so hot. *Anna Karenina* makes death look sexy."

Some of the girls buried their faces in their books. Others twirled their hair and chewed at the end of their ribbons. Most of the girls had not heard of *Anna Karenina*; it was the word "sexy" that flamed their cheeks. Hot was as close as they could get to whatever form of impurity Anntell Briar was flinging in the air about some Russian woman. By the looks on their faces, Anntell knew there would be another gathering in the hopscotch square. She chuckled at the thought of it.

Then she spoke directly to Alfie. "I'll bet you've read this novel. If you haven't, I can lend it to you."

Alfie smiled. "It's Tolstoy's best work. I've read it twice."

"Well excuse me, Mr. Johns! I'm interested in the character of Anna. I'm not into old men, and they'll never be into me. All women who cheat have earned that new pair of arms around them." Her face contoured like a cobra set to strike on *Anne of Green Gables* and the *Bobbsey Twins*.

A ripple of laughter and hoots came from the older boys. Some of the girls coughed so loudly they sounded in the throes of an asthma attack. The teacher returned, her face on the verge of collapse. She glanced quickly at Anntell Briar and was glad to see she was still in her seat.

She didn't want a confrontation; she knew the girl was much smarter than she, herself, could ever be. Sending her to the principal was out of the question. She'd seen how the old fool looked at Anntell Briar, and secretly stuffed his high blood-pressure pill under his tongue like a piece of forbidden chewing gum in the presence of this dark beauty.

5

DUNCAN BRIAR CAUGHT Arthur's eye in the rearview mirror as they were returning from church. Arthur sat in the back seat with his sister, who had her eye on something outside the window or was pretending she'd discovered an interest. He could see the back of her hat pushed to the side of her head. For a moment he had an urge to whip it off her head and fling it out the window. His mother sat passively in the front seat with her hat pinned securely with a long pin. An oyster-coloured ball, at the end of the pin, resembled a smooth wad of chewing gum.

Arthur's attraction to hats was a way of avoiding his father's eye. The old man had something on his mind and it would come at him at any time.

"Arthur, are you that lazy that it would kill you to pick up a stick. I told you twice to pick up the wood in front of the garage and put it where it belongs."

A deadly silence filled the black coupe. Rosie Briar's head tilted forward as her gloved hand slipped her white hankie from under her sleeve. She hated these verbal attacks on Arthur, but knew her intervention would make things even worse for him. Anntell continued to look out the window in silence. Her father would not plan an attack on her; they were too much alike. And she was too verbally quick for him. He had his target, her brother Arthur.

"Did you hear what I said, or are you as backward as you appear?" A soft moan came from the back of Rosie's throat. Feminine moans excited Duncan; when her throat betrayed her, his wife was at her most vulnerable.

Arthur felt his blood coming through his veins like dirty water through a pump, but he refused to answer the idiot behind the wheel. He looked at his mother whose head was bent forward. There was no use in answering the old man. Arthur had figured out his father's game plan, the old bastard did nothing without a plan. He could see the bulging veins in the back of his neck, and the heat of anger crawling around the rim of his ears.

Arthur cupped his hands over his mouth to choke back a sarcastic smile. Men his old man's age had heart attacks in the heat of anger—one couldn't come fast enough for Duncan Briar. He'd already had one heart attack and was on medication. Duncan had something else on his mind; his hand on his flesh for the ready. Arthur would not go head to head with him in front of his mother. She'd have enough of him to deal with later. The idea of his father using his beautiful mother so carnally enraged Arthur. How humiliating for her to have to stop dancing, to have the music ripple out of her veins and listen to the swollen darkness around her. And when Duncan finished with her, she would be too tired to try a new step.

They turned into the driveway before Duncan could finish his attack on Arthur. He looked over at his wife and lifted her head with a tug of his hand. She was as compliant as a leaf. Duncan Briar smiled. Arthur got out of the car and opened the door for his mother. He could feel the tremble in her slight body as he escorted her into the house.

"Don't answer him back! You're a bigger man than he is!" His mother leaned into him and barely whispered.

He heard his father's voice rise behind them. "You better clean out that damned slop pail, and make sure Joseph uses it before you wash it out now! And get rid of that wood!"

Anntell removed her hat and made her way up the stairs. In her room, she could hear very little of her family's voices below her. In the world she loved best, Anna Karenina listened for the sound of a train.

Rosie went into her bedroom to get her Sunday apron. Her head throbbed as she emerged into the pantry to prepare Sunday dinner. She'd put the roast in the oven before she left for church, and had already made dessert on Saturday. The radio was playing in the kitchen, soft chuckles coming between voices as her mother listened to *Amos and Andy*.

She longed to get dinner over with so she could go to Joseph, sweet, gentle Joseph, and sing to him in peace. She couldn't look in on him before dinner. Joseph would be too excited and want her to stay at his side, to hold him up to the window and play a game of hand shadows along the wall.

Duncan brought in the cooked roast from the oven and placed it on a platter before his wife.

"I like my meat just right, Rosie. I don't suppose I have to remind you; you've known my tastes for years, have you not?"

Rosie reached for her best carving knife from the block and stood looking down at the dark roast in front of her. She imagined her husband on the platter. Fully cooked. She knew exactly what she would carve into with the slick blade. She sliced deeply into the edge of the meat. Its warm juice trickled through her fingers. She wasn't aware that she was crying until she wiped her cheek and caught a glimpse of her face in the mirror about the sink. Smears of juice covered her pale face like blush.

She knew exactly what he was referring to under his twisted smile. She winced when he put his spotted hands under her apron and opened two buttons down low on her dress. His heavy breathing swam along her neck like a dirty limerick. She could hear the sound of loud laughter coming from the radio as her mother turned up the volume to distract Duncan out of the pantry. Rosie knew her mother sensed what he was up to, and had sent out a warning in her defence. Duncan swore under his breath as he stormed out past Isla and down the hall. She could hear the bedroom door slam, its anger echoing along the hall.

Arthur made his way to the back room and looked down at his sleeping brother, stretched out on the planks with a slight smile on his slim face. He decided not to wake Joseph as he draped his quilt over him. The room had cooled down with the rain, and Arthur closed the window near the sleeping boy. He knew his mother would be in after dinner to see to Joseph and would be alarmed that he could catch his death of cold. He did not want to add to her misery. The old man would be around the house all day; no chance he'd be off to the neighbours to play cribbage on a Sunday.

Arthur removed the pail and made his way to the washroom to empty it and run it under hot water. He was the only member in the house allotted this chore. Anntell outright refused.

"I'm not going around here smelling like an out-house."

It was an impossible task for his grandmother, and his mother was forbidden to carry the pail. His father made his message clear.

"This is not a job for you, Rosie, and if you insist, I will cart him off to the asylum—where everyone else deposits kids like him, where I wanted to put him all along."

His own contempt for what he had created, what spill of his sexual pleasure he had filled his wife with, meant he entered Joseph's room rarely. It was enough that he had to look at Arthur, listless and weak. His son was nothing like him. When he had been Arthur's age, his plans were made. He could build anything. Duncan believed he had his hands wrapped around the future, had the golden goose by the neck. He trained himself to believe that grief could be stunted by hard work. He turned himself into a warrior of discipline.

He was certain Arthur would amount to nothing. His mind didn't run in a solid direction. He would end up a charity case. His would be a life of odd jobs. In another two years he'd probably take off somewhere, if his mother couldn't talk him into other plans. She could always use Joseph as an ace up her sleeve.

Anntell was different. She fought with her mind. She could knock the hinges off any door with her intellect and beauty. At times, the way she turned her head, he could see his father's twinkle in her eyes, just like when he'd walked along the shore with him as a young boy.

Arthur heard his father go into his bedroom down the hall and close the door. He would read or watch television until someone called him to the dinner table. Arthur returned from the washroom with the pail just as Joseph stirred from his sleep and looked up at him. He picked him up and sat him on the pail in the corner. Arthur watched him and wondered what the hell was wrong with him. Why had he not grown like other kids? Nobody ever mentioned what his condition was called, if they even knew. Arthur believed that Joseph understood more than he let on. Joseph had one advantage over him with their old man: he never had to speak to Duncan.

Arthur rarely spoke to Joseph—it would have been easier to communicate with a cat—but today he told him that his mama would be down to feed him soon. The boy folded his hands playfully. He understood what his brother said to him. Arthur didn't hate his brother; he hated the man who brought him into this world, a shell that he didn't care to fill in. Arthur noticed his brother's behaviour was different on this day. Joseph kept a steady gaze on the geranium window. And when Arthur lifted him off of the pail, Joseph refused to move his hands from his mouth for Arthur to put his sweater over his head. His bony hands moved in slow, straight strides across his mouth and produced the strangest of sounds, sounds he had never heard before. Arthur patted him on the head. "Are you playing games with me, Joseph? You know mama doesn't want you to be cold." Joseph stroked his brother's face with his hand as Arthur slipped his sweater carefully over his head.

6

ROSIE'S MOTHER, ISLA Jones, had exceptional hearing. She needed it. She went blind at thirty-nine from an illness that swept up to her front porch, past her beautiful roses, stealing their colours as it roamed, then sneaked in through her screen door. The intruder found Isla at the table sewing white cotton into a summer dress for her daughter, Rosie.

She described the illness to the doctors. The white material she was sewing turned into a patch of dark grey fog in her hands. The fog got darker and darker, and never went away. She attributed her hazy vision, the severe pain and the rainbows that surrounded her eyes, to late nights of sewing. It came with its own name: glaucoma. Her hearing became her map to daily living.

At thirty-nine, she was a widow with a seventeen-year-old daughter with one year of schooling to go before graduation. Her husband had passed away years before from the black lung. Practical women get things going. Isla had wooden rails put in all around the walls of her small bungalow. She used them as guides to each room. She understood, as a practical woman would, that her livelihood had come to an end. Her little sewing business could be no longer. Her nephew, who had a family of his own and was living and working in the United States, sent money each month, but things were still a great struggle. Rosie tried to do her share. She could manage some of the housework and some of the sewing, but there were meals to prepare and yard work that always needed to be done.

Duncan Briar had been one of Isla's steady customers. Isla had never cared for the man and his peculiar ways around women. He seemed to sift through them like paper, still waiting for the right page upon which to leave his signature. He was arrogant and demanding.

"Mother wants this dress hemmed to her liking," he ordered on one of his first visits to her shop. Isla took the silk dress in her hands and turned over the hem where his mother had marked it for cutting. She smiled to herself. She'd have liked to hem the damn thing around Rowena Briar's neck. Stitch by stitch.

When he returned a few days later to pick up the dress, he examined the hem like a surgeon checking his work. He ran his hand along the fine stitching before asking Isla to put it on the hanger and in the bag he'd brought. The following week, he arrived with two more dresses to be hemmed. He made no comment about the silk dress. Isla refused to ask about it. She did not have to seek approval from the Briar family about her work. On his third visit, he brought along two pairs of suit pants to be hemmed for himself. He always examined the finished work, bowed his head, paid, and left a satisfied customer.

Isla soon became suspicious about Duncan Briar's many visits. They had become weekly visits. She'd seen the way he looked at her daughter. What would he bring in next to be hemmed? His dog's tail? He had shown no interest in Isla, who was closer to his age. He was a confirmed bachelor in his late thirties, a man of wealth, a shipbuilder, who did not care to spend much time around the mill, although he still owned the business. Why did he still live with his mother? Something was amiss.

Duncan and Isla had not attended the same school. As a young man, he was never seen at the dances in the community. Few people had ever seen him with a lady friend. He was always off to one country or another. Rowena Briar decided, in her later years, that there were other places to see in this world and began to take trips abroad herself.

Rosie Jones did not return to school. The challenges caused by her mother's blindness were too much to deal with along with her studies. Duncan Briar hemmed in on the situation. He'd watched the dark beauty Rosie Jones emerge from the rose garden with a basket of flowers. She kept her mother surrounded with the scent of wild daises and buttercups and tiger lilies, and the sturdy lupines that marched around their property.

Duncan Briar watched her tired limbs as she slowly made her way up the stairs to the front door. She had grown weary since her mother's blindness, and with this weariness she had bloomed into a woman. Her face had the deepened maturity that comes from unexpected sorrow and worry. All her visions of her mother being able to watch her graduate, watch her walk down the aisle in the gown she would have fashioned for her wedding, see her grandchildren run and play, all of them were lost to the grey fog.

Duncan saw Rosie's predicament as something that could be beneficial to him. His mother, Rowena, needed a personal aid for her daily grooming, a perfumed watchdog so to speak. Isla Jones had trained her daughter well. She could sew, and mix and match the latest fashions of the day. There would be no housekeeping duties required of the girl. His mother was enough to dust off. She was more difficult than ever these days.

Duncan sat with his mother for dinner. Rowena was terse but brittle in her brown two-piece suit. She had lost a noticeable amount of weight. Her suit jacket crawled over her shoulders like loose mud sliding over a cliff. She forgot the names of people and places. She stared out towards the backyard with a cup in her hand.

"Do you see that large pool of water out there, Duncan?"

"It's a puddle, Mother; it's always there after a heavy rain."

"Well, I'll be damned; I thought I had gotten rid of it. Do you suppose there is anything in it? I believe I saw something moving around and around in it."

"There's nothing but the wind."

"See, it's moving again. Duncan, why can't you see it?"

A small puddle was marooned between two fence posts.

"Can you see it?"

"Yes, Mother. I can see it clearly."

"What's moving around in the bloody thing?"

"An alligator," he added sarcastically. "He lived in that puddle years ago."

"Who would put a radiator out there?"

"It's nothing, Mother; I told you it is nothing, just the wind."

"I must be going daft in the head, seeing things that don't exist. But I did see that pool of water stir, Duncan. I saw what I saw. I'll take my rest now. Perhaps I shall see things more clearly when I am refreshed."

Duncan Briar walked out into the backyard near the puddle and looked up at his father's bedroom window. The drapes were closed over. He remembered a summer day when his father called down to him. He held his pipe in his hand out the window. The swirl of smoke that hid his father's face intrigued Duncan's five-year-old imagination.

"How are things in the mighty kingdom, my son?" Charlie Briar called out.

"No enemies around; you can come down to the fort."

Duncan saw his mother out on the northern balcony, listening to his exchange with his father. His small voice rose like a balloon about to burst. His mother was wearing a green dress with wide straps over her shoulders. Her hair and face were partially hidden by a large straw-brimmed hat. She held one hand on her hip as she listened to the conversation between her husband and son.

Duncan saw his father come around the corner of the house with a plate of sandwiches and sweets, and two jars of cold lemonade the cook had made for them. His father had placed a small wooden table and two chairs in the fort. Warriors needed nourishment, he'd said. They had only just sat down to eat when he heard his mother shout to his father to bring the child in for a proper lunch. His father pretended not to hear her; she shouted a second time, more loudly. He could see the redness in his father's face, and the way his eyes looked when they turned towards the balcony. They were frozen eyes, frozen on his mother, on her commands, frozen over with his hatred for her. It was all there. He didn't say one word to his wife. Just nodded for Duncan to leave the fort and go into lunch with his mother.

Duncan walked over to the puddle between the two fence posts and swirled his shoe into the clear water. At thirty-seven years of age, he realized how much he missed and loved his father, and how much he hated his mother.

What happened with his father down at the brook had been brewing for a long time. And what happened had been covered up by his mother. His father's body was found by an old friend from the mill on his way to work. The bullet's penetration was minimal. He'd bled to death. Rowena had the rifle destroyed and swore the friend to secrecy. He and two other workers helped carry his body from the path and cleared up the aftermath of Charlie Briar's agony. Cause of death: a drunken fall, a heart attack.

This was old news to Duncan. He'd overheard his mother and the mill worker whom she had driven almost mad with shame and regret.

"I always liked Mr. Briar," said the worker, his hands working themselves into a sweat. "He was good to me and my family. I don't like lying to people. It wasn't what I was brought up to do. I know it wasn't the liquor that took its revenge out on your husband's heart."

"What would you know about a heart attack when

you can barely punctuate a sentence?" Rowena Briar's voice trembled with rage.

"I know it was no heart attack, Missus. Mr. Briar aimed that rifle to his heart and I believe that he changed his mind, came to his senses for the boy's sake, but the gun went off somehow and grazed his chest deep enough for the poor man to bleed to death. I don't like having to tell people he died from liquor blowing up his heart for the sake of my job. There are many things that can tinker with a man's heart."

The man had beaten Rowena Briar down; his words fell on her like a torrent of freezing rain. She saw the truth in what he said, and the idea of it enraged her even more. She was aware of his sentiment, although she herself could not and would not live with it. The idea of it deflated her like a flat tire. Charlie was dead. She hadn't pulled the trigger. Facts can and do outweigh sentiment any day in her mind.

His mother made her way into the parlour after her rest. She wore two different slippers on her feet.

"What are you doing at your age playing in puddles, Duncan? I saw you out there."

He looked towards his mother. As if for the first time in his life, he saw her as she always had been—proud, defiant, prying, and unloving. She was a stew simmered with the wrong ingredients, devoid of flavour. She had been a beauty in her day; she was still handsome in the way old flesh can be sculpted by defiance and money.

"I'm going to hire a young girl, Mother, to help you with your daily grooming."

She looked at Duncan, displeasure on her face.

"You'll do no such thing. What do you think I am, some sort of poodle?"

Duncan looked at his mother, his eyes icy. He was not going to turn into his father. He was going to speak up the way his father should have done. She stared back at him without a word.

"I'm going to ask young Rosie Jones if she'd be interested in the position. I know she's not returning to school due to her mother's illness. She can use the money."

Rowena Briar opened her jaw like a reluctant child required to swallow bitter medicine.

"You are referring to that cripple, the girl with the blind mother? That's just what I'll require taking care of my needs. What do you suppose she can do for me all day, sit around and sew?"

Duncan Briar's voice angered. "For starters, Mother, she can put a matching pair of slippers on your snarled snake feet. She can dress you properly, so you don't go about looking like a scarecrow left out in the rain too long. "

Rowena Briar looked down at her feet as Duncan walked briskly out of the parlour and out the front door.

Rosie Jones was out in the front garden when he arrived at her house and parked his car at the gate.

"I hear you are not returning to school this fall." He stood back and waited for her reply.

Something churned in his stomach and crawled up into his chest. He was uneasy with his approach. He should have asked how her mother was doing and how things were going for them. Why did he have to be so businesslike with her, when other feelings were chewing away at his insides?

His mouth watered up. Rosie wore a frost-coloured apron over her white printed dress. He imagined the material melting away in the sun and exposing her pure virginal flesh. The wind drifted under her dress and she fought it off as if it were a wasp attack. Her hands were swift as she tucked the material between her legs. She had dropped her basket at her feet.

"Are you here to see my mother, Mr. Briar?"

He swallowed hard before he made his pitch to the beautiful young woman, pushing his hands deep into his side pockets.

"I need someone to do small chores for my mother. Take care of her grooming. You know, woman things, nails and hair, picking outfits for her to wear. She's getting somewhat forgetful. I can have someone pick you up and take you home. And I'll make the wages worth your while."

Rosie thanked him politely. She watched his hands

flapping. A pair of wild wings in his pockets, but hesitated to ask if he had been stung by a bee.

"I will have to discuss this with my mother. She's not well enough at the moment to be left alone for a day. I will have to wait until she's on the mend to discuss this with her."

"Take your time! I'll come by in a few weeks. Maybe we can work something out by then."

Duncan Briar sat behind the wheel of his car before turning the ignition. He realized that Rosie had seen his hands flapping like a freshly caught mackerel on a wharf. The bewildered look on her face assured him that she wasn't aware of his attraction to her. Her innocence was part of what drew him to her.

7

ALFIE JOHNS SAT at the dining-room table as Bertha prepared dinner and outlined Joseph Briar's small frame in his mind. How much could the boy eat? Was he ever brought to the table to share a meal with his family? Perhaps he was permitted to sit in a highchair at his mother's side. Alfie doubted this very much. It would be too messy for his father to stomach.

Where did the blind grandmother sit at Duncan Briar's table? Poor Rosie Briar, with her brace on her foot—was she allotted a seat of honour? No doubt Arthur ate like an ostrich with his head close to his food; Anntell would be at one head of the table, away from the others, with her long hands scooping up potatoes with a silver spoon. A child digging in soft snow.

Duncan Briar would take full advantage of the family in front of him—they who relied on his food in their stomachs, his roof over their heads, the clothes he paid for on their backs, the hatred for him in their hearts. He could sit back and take inventory of his generosity, while they mocked it and cleaned their plates. He could cleanse his own wounds with theirs. They were ungrateful. He had let Rosie keep what she considered another "son"; her mother was under his roof. He put up with Arthur and his endless ingratitude; Arthur, who'd rather sulk and feel sorry for the stupor life left him than face the world like a man. He was the son of a wealthy man. What more did he need? Duncan had to be hard on him. Arthur's uncanny resemblance to Rowena Briar made matters worse. Whenever he turned and looked at Arthur, his dead mother looked back at him, with hatred in her eyes.

Yes, even his beautiful, precocious Anntell, with her gypsy spirit, despised him. She looked like her mother, but had inherited Rowena Briar's tongue. She would have preferred a younger man for her mother, he was aware of that. His rules were never laid down for her. Anntell would be fussy about who she'd lie down with; he was sure of her direction in life. He envied her youth, her blunt opinions, her stunning beauty.

Duncan Briar looked over at his wife. Before they were married, he had made love to several women in his travels from Hong Kong to Berlin. From London to Paris, from Sweden to Amsterdam, these women screamed in his sprawling embrace. He returned to Rocky Point with several accents spilling from his ears.

Yet he had not had the privilege of a woman like Rosie. She came to him like a pet lamb. At one call, her soft body void of any womanly fuss. She never once complained. When she sighed, it was he who wanted to scream, he who wanted to pour every ounce of air from his lungs into hers.

Bertha and Wilfred Johns sat at their table facing each other over the spread in front of them. Alfie sat in the middle, close to the dining-room window. This was always the seating arrangement on Sundays in the Johns' house. The rest of the week they ate at the long kitchen table. Alfie concentrated on the chicken in front of him. It looked smaller than the chicken Bertha usually cooked on a Sunday. She never knew who would drop by to feast at her table.

Joseph's hands flickered in front of Alfie's eyes. The frailty of their structure at odds with the job he imposed on them. Alfie imagined them like small breaths of wind composing a new melody. He refused the chicken leg offered to him; he wasn't really hungry. Bertha was annoyed that anyone, especially Alfie, who would probably be chewing on a piece of cold bologna for a meal if that mother of his had kept him, would refuse her cooking. Alfie caught her look and stared back at her. He knew what she was thinking: how lucky he was to be with her and Wilfred. Well-fed and well-dressed, despite his illegitimacy. Bertha had a fear of wayward girls, especially beautiful ones like Anntell Briar and Alfie's biological mother.

"Did I hear your friend say that the Briars had a third child?"

Bertha coughed and looked over at her husband for support. She lowered her eyes to her plate and continued to eat away at the chicken.

"God knows, nobody has ever seen a third child. How could anyone have a child and keep it hidden?"

Alfie smiled in her direction. He had hit checkmate on this one.

"Tell me, how *can* anyone have a child and keep such a thing hidden?"

Bertha coughed loudly, then guzzled down a glass of water. Alfie was persistent.

"There have been rumours. And I heard your friend tell you the story. Where did your friend get her information?"

Wilfred stopped eating and looked over at Alfie.

"Nobody wants to go around messing into Duncan Briar's life; the man is ruthless. He employs half of the village. He's the kind of man you have to pretend to like. People don't question what goes on behind his door. "

Bertha, with a piece of chicken caught between her teeth, spoke up. She looked over at Alfie and gave her own opinion of the Briars.

"I know you have to go to school with his kids. But stay away from them. That girl is wayward. I'm surprised she's not in the family way yet, the way she trots around the village. And that poor boy of theirs is as dumb as a bundle of kindling. There's something brewing in his eyes that he'll unleash on somebody one of these days."

Alfie sideswiped Bertha's assumptions and spoke directly to her.

"Anntell Briar has a brilliant mind. She's extremely well read and has her own opinions, but I've yet to hear of her being wayward. If truth be known, men want to chase her. And there is nothing stupid about Arthur Briar."

Red-faced, Bertha Johns threw down her napkin. "I know a wayward girl when I see one, and she fits the bill. You mark my word. If I had it my way, I'd lock girls like her up in a work farm and teach them how to make dumplings instead of poor illegitimate babies. And I hope you haven't any ideas of leading her down to the river."

"I'll never tell," Alfie bit down on his tongue. He'd almost called her "Bertha." He preferred not to address them in any manner; he did not like either Bertha or Wilfred Johns. He longed for his real family, wherever they were.

Bertha looked over at her husband, who kept his head down. She had caught his eyes buried into that wayward girl's flesh on more than one occasion. God knows what else he would have liked to bury himself into, had she not been beside him. She had never said a word to him. She knew trouble when she saw it. And he had admitted to the wrath one might encounter by interfering with anything that belonged to Duncan Briar. It was probably nothing but fear that kept him faithful to Bertha.

Alfie excused himself before leaving the table. He saw no need to keep goading them; he would leave home as soon as he graduated. Bertha's voice was a hill of contempt, a bump in the road hit without warning. Alfie, although always different, was never as formidable as he appeared to her now.

"Where do you think you're going, Alfie, with my meal still on the table in front of you?"

"I'm going to find out if my birth mother can make dumplings. I'm betting she can."

He heard Bertha's fork drop as he walked out of the dining room, a rumble of conversation behind him as he went out the back door. Bertha's voice an icicle about to crash.

"The nerve of that boy to want to go looking for his real mother. It's a disgrace, after all I've done for him. What am I, Wilfred, a chicken leg?"

"Who the hell told him he was adopted, Bertha?"

"How do I know? He'd be too slow to figure it out himself. It will have been that Briar girl. She's got an opinion on everything. She'd roll that out to him like a piecrust. "

Alfie walked into the village and bought himself a

soda at the Corner Restaurant with a smile on his lips. In the distance he heard the sounds of slow moving traffic. It was almost noon. The Briar family would be having dinner at the end of their silver forks.

Anntell sank her fork into another piece of roast and raised it to her mouth, but not before noticing the clean deep cut in the meat.

"Delicious as ever, Mother, but you could have sliced someone's throat with that cut."

She had started calling her "Mother" ever since she got into what she referred to as "heavy reading." "Mama" sounded too juvenile for her. Arthur could call her "Mama" forever if he liked; he probably would, he kept so close to her hem. She couldn't care one way or the other.

Rosie Briar did not answer her daughter. She asked Arthur politely if he would mind checking on his grandmother. Isla requested to stay in the kitchen for her meals. She had not mapped Duncan Briar's house out like she had done when she and Rosie lived in their own little home. She had cursed her darkness once and never repeated the curse again. She knew her daughter was here, not because she wanted to be, but because of the crisis they had had to face.

Isla Jones did not want any part of this house, or of Duncan Briar for that matter. What she did, she did for her dear child. She could deal with losing her sight, but not with losing Rosie. Isla heard footsteps approaching from the dining room. She could tell by the heavy tread that Arthur was in the kitchen. He came closer and bent down near his grandmother.

"Do you need anything else, Grandma?" His voice was uneven. A piece of ice at the edge of a cliff.

Isla reached out and took his hands in hers.

"You are a good lad, Arthur. Remember that, and believe it!"

"It's too bad the old man doesn't think so. He won't leave me alone. Anntell can get away with anything."

"You have to concentrate on leaving yourself alone, child. You'll be out on your own before you know it. Getting what you want can be destructive. That's a lesson Anntell might learn the hard way."

Arthur shrugged his shoulders and returned to the dining room. Even wisdom seemed to escape through the seams of the Briar household.

"Grandma doesn't need anything else." He mumbled to his mother.

Isla knew that her grandson was very troubled. She could feel it in the way he buried his father's verbal abuse deep inside the silence of his own world, storing away its damage. It affected everything in his life. He had no friends, and if he did, he could not bring them here because his father forbade him to bring anyone to his house.

Duncan Briar hadn't anticipated Arthur's revenge,

displaced and childish as it was. His resolutions were formed in anger, his revenge in reverse. He had set up a small business right under Duncan's nose, bringing those he thought his friends to a window in the Briar home. Displaying the thing his father most wanted hidden. In truth, it was his father he wanted to put on display. But Arthur had not counted on the fact that his father's intelligence far outweighed his own emotions, and that the geranium window would be his downfall.

8

IN 1900, DUNCAN Briar watched his father's casket being lowered into the wet ground and wept. He was ten years old, an only child, and believed weeping was required at a funeral, especially one for a relative. He rarely broke the rules, and proved to himself that one did not get anything wrong in front of a crowd. He had a first-class mind in a first-class house. He yearned for love in that first-class house, and when it didn't come, he decided a loving home was an illusion, like Santa Claus who sank down the chimney. He wanted for nothing that a brilliant mind could provide with a bit of muscle.

His mother's strong hand gripped him by the shoulder. She whispered in his ear. "Shut-up, or you'll end up as weak as your father. Take a look at where you could end up before your time!"

Duncan wiped his eyes immediately. A rather large puddle pooled close to the open grave. For a brief moment the child imagined an alligator close by, but the alligator had vanished, years ago.

That was the last day he ever wept as a child. Where do a child's tears go when he no longer cries? Duncan had thought about this when he felt the painful longing for his father. He always wiped his dry eyes. It was the sign of a warrior. This was probably what his father would have told him.

He watched his mother's cold eyes circle the mourners. They rested on crooked coat hems and the bad hair fashions on some of the red-eyed women gathered like crows for a feast. The men were not much more presentable in their outdated overcoats and worn-down shoes. They were frightful in appearance, she thought.

Rowena Briar did not know any of them by name, nor did she care to find out their names. These were the sort of people her husband Charlie dealt with at the mill, through sawdust and strife. She was not about to converse with people who scattered their vowels like chicken feed and who confused sentiment for knowledge. She had nothing in common with them. She knew what they were thinking by the looks on their dull faces, and did not accept sorrow in the traditional sense. Crying for the dead was an outcry for oneself.

Few people spoke to her. They kept their distance, but now and again glanced at the child's dry face with great pity. The Briar family owned and operated the successful sawmill in Rocky Point. They employed many people from the village and from surrounding areas for miles around. Men built their homes from the lumber sawed at the Briars' mill. New church steeples rose through the fog of Rocky Point and hid in the night sky. Wood shaped from the Briars' saws covered bridges and built up schools. Breakwaters endured the heavy seas under their finely cut lumber.

Charlie Briar was a fine wrap of a man who spoke quietly and respectfully to people. He was well liked and respected by all his workers. His greatest weakness came to him in a manner it befalls many wealthy men. He loved beauty for beauty's sake, in women and in art. When he was a bachelor, works of art arrived in concealed packages to his door and were hung around his house for his own pleasure. He loved to collect the dust from foreign countries on his heels. By the time he returned to Rocky Point, he had washed away the dust and replaced it with sawdust on his work boots. He refused to brag to anyone about his little rests on distant shores. He passed out souvenirs to all his workers.

Many of his mill workers, with large families, could barely afford a trip to Halifax across the ferry on the Canso Strait. If illness was involved, he spared no expense for them or their families. He paid the shot by train to transport them to their destination and back home again.

Things began to change for Charlie Briar when he married Rowena Stewart, a teacher at the nearby school. She had graduated from the Teachers' College in Truro and accepted a position in Rocky Point for the fall season. She was tall and elegant in stature. Her red hair, when not in a bun, was a flame in his hands. She corrected his adjectives and adverbs on the sandy beach of Rocky Point. He believed nouns and verbs were all connected by the alphabet. English was his least favourite subject in or out of school, he chuckled. He proposed by carving "wount you marry me" in the sand. Rowena hated waste on fantasy and sentiment. Their courtship was brief.

They travelled to Aberdeen, Scotland, on their honeymoon, had their photo taken with two Black Angus bulls, to remind them, at Rowena's request, that they, together, were a pair in life. Charlie Briar looked at his wife on their honeymoon in her Stewart flannel nightgown with a crest on its yoke, and wondered if he had just made love to a flag. She fluttered lightly, went limp, then rolled over to face the slight breeze coming from an open draft with a smile covered by a flame of red hair.

His workers noticed dramatic changes in his character a few months later. He grew moody and restless. Concealed in his desk was a flask of hard liquor to soften his days. He lost interest in the business and soon they had to deal with his wife at the helm. But business flourished under her stern fist and demanding orders. Rowena could be heard lecturing her husband on more than one occasion on the merits of hard work. He often arrived to work late and left early. She had his desk moved to a small office down the hall from hers.

From its window, Charlie Briar watched the smoke rise from the mill and be carried off by the wind beyond the mountains in the distance, his empire going up in smoke. He believed that his son, Duncan, would be his saving grace. His mind cast back to a time and place when he and Rowena could have possibly conceived a child. He slept in another room and could not remember having been seduced by tartan in quite a while.

Charlie studied the child's innocent face for a trace of Rowena. Happy that the child looked like him, he picked him up and whispered in his ear with great delight.

"You are a true blue-blooded Briar, son."

He quit drinking, and worshipped the young lad who followed at his heels like a pair of tracks. Duncan longed to walk along the shore and down to the brook with his father. They gathered fossils and sand dollars down by the sea. They carried home buckets of sand for the sandbox that Charlie had built in the backyard. It became their fort, and they stayed in it for hours, imagined warriors at its edges, alligators in the rain puddles a few feet away; a stray tomcat turned lion basking in the sun, and squirrels big as dragons roared above in the trees. And Queen Rowena, in her castle, on the northern balcony, looked down and made plans to do away with this nonsense. This was Charlie's private war with the queen of Rocky Point. This enemy he did not acknowledge to his son, and this enemy he could not keep at bay.

It was a warm September day when Duncan Briar started school, at six years of age, with his mother at his side. She clutched a list of instructions for the young teacher. Her son was not to be given idiom for reading material. No moral antiquities that hindered real thinking in the brains of young children were to be set upon Duncan Briar. He was not to play with snot-infested children at recess or share his nourishing lunch with them in exchange for a molasses sandwich or a tea biscuit. His refined grammar was to be maintained at all cost, and should he come home using words like "yip" and "frig off" and "I dunno," the school would have Rowena's input, in proper English, in no uncertain terms, and her financial donations would be terminated.

Young Duncan Briar made his way around the school desks, past a knot of boys to the classroom window when his mother finally left. In the distance, he watched smoke billow from his father's mill. He smiled as he imagined him waiting for him in the fort. He had warned his father to be careful of the alligators and the dragons while he was gone. The lion was too old to do anything but sleep. But unbeknownst to the boy, the queen in the castle was not asleep. She stood on her balcony as the two men she hired dismantled the hideous eyesore below her. While Charlie Briar stood behind the drapes of his bedroom window and waited for the lion to roar.

"Where were you, Father, when the enemy attacked, where were you?" Suddenly, Duncan realized his father was not as brave as he pretended. He had lied to him, had let their fort fall before his eyes when he could have called upon the alligators and dragons to do battle with him. Duncan no longer went on their treasure hunts for sand dollars or fossils. They, too, might disappear under his father's watch. Having lost his magical world, Duncan grew sullen and withdrawn.

A hatred bloomed in Charlie Briar's chest, savage and dark. He wanted to hire the two men who dismantled the fort to dismantle Rowena Stewart. His son stayed away from him. Their kingdom had fallen. They ate meals together like strangers at an elegant restaurant. The child spoke to his mother in perfect English; his mother congratulated him on his excellent grammar as she nodded slowly towards her husband, slumped over his plate at the end of the table. After school, she started taking Duncan to the mill with her and introducing him to the business world. At nine, he discussed business like he'd once discussed his fairytale world.

Once in a while Charlie could still see that wonder in his child's eyes when Duncan looked at puddles or up into the tall trees. He longed to tell him the truth, but knew the consequences would have been fatal. She'd have him sell the mill and would leave with his son. He'd be the real monster in his son's eyes. The only thing he could trust was that she would do anything for revenge.

Rowena Stewart's marriage to Charlie Briar fell at her feet in a heap of dust. He was too soft to be held like a real man should be held. She couldn't be bothered to tell him so. She was much smarter than he ever could be. He'd prefer to play cards with his low-caste workers than engage in a game of chess with her. His imagination was alive in puddles and tall trees and poor grammar. He had never grown up. The business would have failed if it weren't for her iron fist. What she could not admit to herself, would never say out loud, was that she had been rejected by him. He had probably never really loved her, not the way she loved him.

Why did he even bother to marry her? The thought often crossed her mind. She had never before been rejected by a member of the opposite sex. Despite it all, she loved him more than she ever had when his hands accidently touched her shoulders as he walked around her chair. His touch was seductive, even playful around the child. This was his way of hurting her, letting her know how handy he could be to the touch when the child was watching, when proper English was not required. His handsome face stung her with its smile.

He sat across from her and watched sweat build up under her bangs. He watched the sweat melt down her face, over her nose, form a wet moustache above her quivering lip until she drowned the beads in her linen napkin. Other things happened in her body. Small grenade explosions in the pit of her stomach, sending debris down to her toes, scorching as it rippled between her thighs. Her darling bastard of a husband watched it all, and offered her a steaming oyster on the end of his fork dipped in vinegar.

In private, a few years back, she could tell by the way his hands gripped the edge of her body, the way he crawled along it carefully as if he were examining the edge of a blunt saw at the mill, feeling for jagged edges when they did make love. The nerve of him to love the child that came from her after such manhandling. Rowena Briar swallowed the idea of it, why she had even consented to a mauling from a pit bull.

Charlie began to drink again, more than ever. He went to sleep drunk and woke to drink. He asked a trusted worker what was going on down at the mill. He no longer ate meals with the boy. He couldn't bear to see the disdain on his young face; he was convinced the child hated him. But Charlie Briar had one act of courage left. One he planned on his own terms. He walked along the mill path under a full moon, stopped and took one final look at his beloved son's future, the Briar mill. He could smell the sweet scent of freshly cut wood as he walked down to the brook past the mill. The water lapped over the invisible touch of small hands and small feet in rubber boots, a few wet leaves, the streaks of the dancing moon in its ripple, the shadows of dancing curls in its silver rush.

He was too far from the house to see a lamp go on in his bedroom window, too far away to hear the footsteps of his son as he walked over to Charlie's bed, intending to make sure he was tucked in. Duncan had been doing this for weeks, to keep his father from growing too cold in the night. The magic had disappeared from his father's eyes in the last few months, Duncan had seen that and had grown alarmed.

Standing beside his father's empty bed, Duncan heard the sharp report of a gunshot blast, and the murmurs of the brook as it rippled downstream with what was left of his dreams.

And Charlie Briar would never know.

9

ALFIE JOHNS READ through college applications. He weighed carefully his options for his future. He wanted to see the world, gather international experience to add to his portfolio. He might travel for a year and then go to college, but first he would work for a year before hitting the road.

He had graduated, along with Anntell Briar, whom he was sure could not or would not weigh sugar for her tea concerning her future. She was indecisive and restless. Her body quivered when they spoke about their futures. They were down at the shore, their legs hung over the wharf like slim ropes. The July sun played hide and seek behind a swarm of dark clouds from the east.

"Why don't you stay in Rocky Point for another year? I want to work so I can travel before I go on to college. You could travel with me."

Anntell laughed and shrugged her shoulders. "Looks like rain, Alfie. Why don't you travel under the wharf with me?"

He could smell liquor on her breath. She jumped in the water and crawled under the wharf.

"Are you coming or not?" Her voice hummed through the planks on the wharf. She lay full length on the sand.

"Why didn't you bring your camera, Alfie? I'm willing to pose nude for you; consider it a graduation gift."

"You've been drinking, Anntell."

"So what, I can still pose. Your camera wouldn't know the difference."

"It's not a good idea, Anntell. I don't have to take nude photos of you. I prefer natural photography anytime."

She sat up on her knees and pulled him in to her. "What about sex, Alfie? Do you prefer it natural or naughty?"

"You've been drinking; I will not take advantage of this situation." Alfie removed her arms from around him gently.

Anntell came back at him, fire flaming from her mouth. "What in the hell is wrong with you? Have you signed up for a monastery or something? Maybe the cloisters would be a good place for you. You could remain a mute for the rest of your life. You should check into it. And if by chance you get an erection one night, you'll think it's an apparition, and be so scared you won't be able to tell anyone. You will have to point to it. Get to hell out of here, and leave me alone!"

Her black hair hung down over her face. She stood up and began to move her body in a slow circular motion. Anntell removed her blouse and exposed her full breasts. The rest of her clothing slipped off her body like soft snow from a roof. She emerged on the other side of the wharf and stood in the soft rain with her back to him. Alfie thought he heard her weeping.

He left and walked along the shore towards his lane. Once, he turned and looked towards the breakwater to see if Anntell had left and gone home. There was no sign of her along the shore.

Alfie felt an agonizing sense of uncertainty for her. He had, since he was twelve or thirteen, entertained the hope, fantasized, dreamt about a relationship with her. What had stopped him when the opportunity presented itself? He was barely out of his teens; his hormones in overdrive. Yet he could not touch her, could not hurt her in the way his own young mother had been hurt. He may have been the only person who ever loved her enough to say no to her, and mean it for her own safety.

Alfie lay on his bed in the dark. He cursed himself for not going back to check on Anntell. She had taken to rum and coke to quench her thirst. He could see her bronzed body with the soft rain tasting each curve. He angled an imaginary camera in his hand and focused on Anntell's naked body, zoomed in on her back. The curvature of her spine bent forward with the rain dripping down and over its delicate knots imagined the mouth of a warm waterfall christening her body. She had turned her head and looked over her shoulder at him, through him, with malicious sorrow in her eyes. He'd wanted to smile into her eyes, wanted to dissolve what she believed to be a rejection, a displeasure she may have felt in the way she had presented herself, but he changed his mind. He could not have her believe that rain falls to nurture only pain; it falls to nurture growth as well, and it falls on those you love the most.

10

A COLD NOVEMBER tugged at the beginning of December with a deep freeze. Light snow fell from dark clouds. The village of Rocky Point lay in the stark beauty of an Ansel Adams portrait. Arthur was at the back of the house not too far from Joseph's window. He glanced up, noticed little mounds of snow in the geranium cans that resembled the white peaked habits worn by some order of nuns. The shadow of his brother stood behind the frosted window. He could not see his face clearly.

His skates, slung over one shoulder, would be cold when he reached the lake through the path. Arthur knew he would have to make a fire in the drum to warm them up. He reminded himself to keep an eye out for a well-rounded Christmas tree along the route to the lake. He always picked out a nice tree for his mother and brought it home by the middle of December.

Arthur lit up his cigarette. Its smoke bruised the air. He inhaled deeply a whiff of cold air to refresh his lungs. He'd been smoking since he was twelve. Anntell smoked in the house whenever she liked, but he always smoked outdoors. Sometimes she would give him a smoke if she were in the mood.

"Why in the hell don't you buy your own, Arthur?"

"I buy my own, but I ran out. And I won't take advantage of Mama. Besides, I don't have the old man shelling out to me what he gives to you, that's why."

"I can't help it if I'm Father's favourite."

"One of these days, Anntell, you are going to be nobody's favourite."

"You know piss all about me."

"And what do you know about me?"

"You're too passive. You are a lot bigger than the old man is; you have to tell him to shove off. He feasts on weak people. It feeds his control."

"I'm not weak. I'll show him."

"You are so, Arthur, and the old man loves it. He needs people like you. He ignores Joseph and Grandmother because they are vulnerable, but you...you're just weak."

"Joseph can't answer him back, that's why he never bothers with him."

"The truth is, Arthur, Father's jealous of him. Mother showers all her love and affection on Joseph. All that's left for him at night is a worn-out wife at the end of a shift."

"You could help Mama out with Joseph. I never see

you playing with him."

"Why should I? I'm not his mother. I feel sorry for Joseph, but Mother knows what to do for him, how to communicate with him. It's not like I could take him to the store. Besides, he's a distraction for her against the old man."

"It would upset Mama if I fought with Father; she has enough to deal with. She asked me not to answer him back. It would make things worse for me, and for her. How would you like to be married to a man like him?"

Anntell laughed, as hoarse and loud as a high tide.

"Don't hold your breath! It would never happen. I'm sure Mother married out of necessity. She'd have never chosen him if things had been different."

"I know, Anntell. I don't blame Mama. By the way, what's happening with you and Alfie Johns? I suppose you can handle him."

"I'm going to keep him on the edge. Let him have a few more wet dreams before I make my move."

"I know he likes you. I saw the way he looked at you in school."

"We read the same fucking novels, how romantic is that?"

"You sound like the old man."

"He doesn't read novels and neither do you—that's why both of you know so very little about love."

"And your point is?"

"The point is that you are much stronger in math and science than I could ever be. But you need literature to round things out. A few novels under your belt to pump up your imagination, swell up your sex life, if you know what I mean. Now, take your cigarette and get out of my room! I have more reading to do."

Arthur proceeded to the head of the path following his own breath of smoke. He could feel the cold going deeper into his bones as he hurried. He was near the head of the path when he saw his father a few feet ahead of him. He kept walking until they met face to face in the cold white violence of fear.

"Another day of leisure for you, I see, Arthur."

He was surprised to see his father out on a cold day like this.

"I'm going to get a fire going in the drum at the lake and take in a bit of a skating."

"I'm sure you are, you fool. Nobody will come to your freak shows on such a cold day now, will they? You wouldn't dare get a fire going near the window and ruin your stinking little commerce."

Arthur sucked in the cold air and coughed it out.

"I don't know what you are talking about."

"I suspect that is true, in part, like most morons." His father's face was crimson, a combination of anger and the cold. His voice rose and fell like a singer's off key in front of an inattentive audience.

"Your stupidity amuses you, doesn't it? You follow

it everywhere. Can't stand on your own two feet without a quarter in your hand. The hand you would have cut off if I had put you on at the mill. What in the hell is wrong with you? You have my mother's eyes—those horrible things, as if they crawled out of the grave to haunt me. But you certainly lack her insight and her business acumen. She'd be as disgusted by you as I am."

Arthur could feel a pounding in his chest. His head hurt. He swallowed cold air. It felt like a rope was being twisted around his neck by his old man, who had moved even closer to him. The hot steam rising from their mingled breath.

"I am not stupid, Old Man. Don't call me that again! I was always smart enough to know what you were up to. You need the needy in your life to pad your ego. You didn't bother to look beyond the flesh. That's why you never really looked at Joseph."

"What would you call gathering a group of simpletons for a quarter and giving them some cock-and-bull story about a circus? I heard them talking about it in the store yesterday. They couldn't wait to get back here. You put on a good show, they said, the way you got the freak to beat the drum."

Arthur Briar felt a sudden heat crawl up his spine. It pooled around his neck and loosened the feel of a rope.

"I love Joseph, but I can't stand you." He flung the words at his father through the cold air, the blades of his skates close enough to his father's face for a clean shave. Anger provided him his defence. The biting cold made it sharper still.

Duncan Briar stepped back from his son. He would have expected a verbal response from Anntell, but from Arthur? He was suddenly afraid of the boy; he had never really known him—would he be physically violent? No matter, Duncan could not let him get the best of him now.

"Your mother will not be pleased to hear about this. You know how close she is to that *child*." He tried to shout, but the cold choked back his words.

"She will never believe you. She knows I have always loved my brother. I am the only one who helps with him."

Arthur watched his father's face go from crimson to grey. He stammered as he spoke.

"You'll die a helpless fool. And your mother will dent your grave with her knees, praying for and pitying your stupidity."

"What in the hell did you ever do for Joseph?"

"I didn't parade him in front of fools to be laughed at like you did."

"I did it to expose you. *You* deserve it. You are the fool here. I never wanted to hurt Joseph. I wanted people to know just what kind of a cruel fucking idiot you really are."

"I don't have to listen to you and your sewer mouth."

"I've had to listen to yours all my life—you never let up on me."

Duncan Briar took a step towards his son. He reached out to grab Arthur's shoulder, but Arthur was too quick for the old man's grip. He tossed him off. Duncan stumbled and fell backwards along the path. His face convulsed.

Arthur looked down at the face, clammy and pale as a shell. Duncan was sweating like a man under a deep sun. He groaned, then was silent. His pale flesh grew a slight frost, a white stubble where the sweat had been. His lips partially opened, and were tinged blue. He tried to speak but the cold sealed his final words in the vacuum of his throat. And Arthur Briar, too angry to go for help, turned away.

A light snow continued to fall. Duncan Briar's eyes stared upward at the softly falling flakes. He realized his death was going to be much lighter than his life. In the distance between life and death, he was sure he heard the thumping of Joseph's small drum beating like a heart.

Arthur walked away. The silver-crusted lake appeared before him hardened for play. He threw a few branches into an old oil drum and listened to the crackling flames. It had stopped snowing. There were no other people on the lake. He was alone on this dream-like territory. A dark audience of trees and wild animals loomed like snipers in the shadows. Branches hibernated under ice along the path. Overhead, an owl flew low on the hunt.

He laced up and autographed the ice with the blade of his skates. Gliding into his icy world, oblivious to the cold stars, the hidden nocturnal voices, the rabbit destined for death in the owl's claws, he carved a figure eight like a child etching with a sharp pencil. This was his claim to solace, each motion as rewarding as foreplay on the skin of a sheet. It was no secret to him that pain and pleasure covet the same emotions.

He left reluctantly, when the moon began to wane. Cold stars eventually go out. Nocturnal voices fade into dawn's silence. Death is not only a night-time surrender. His father was dead and Arthur Briar had done nothing to help him.

He heard the branches snap under his feet when he left the lake and shuffled towards home. He paused along the path, whisked away snow from a bough, and listened for a new silence.

Duncan Briar's death stirred nothing more than a few shovels and a backhoe in Rocky Point. He was not a well-liked man. When Arthur returned from the lake in the morning, the path was clear. His mother and Anntell were sitting at the kitchen table, dry eyed, making funeral arrangements. The funeral would take place on a Friday. Joseph sat on his grandmother's knees clapping his hands together.

A man taking a short cut home had come across his body. The doctor attributed his death to a heart attack. He had warned Duncan to stay indoors in such cold weather. No one could figure out what he was doing at the edge of the path. Nobody bothered to question Arthur as to why he had been out all night. He had often stayed out on the lake by himself or with others when the ice was frozen.

Arthur was surprised to see a full church for his father's funeral. Alfie Johns sat up close behind the family. Arthur knew he had come for Anntell and his mother's sake. Most of the others came, he presumed, to make sure Duncan Briar was really dead. He doubted if his father had ever spoken a word to many of them.

Anntell invited Alfie back to the house after the burial. Joseph made his way slowly to Alfie and put up his arms. He leaned into Alfie's chest and went to sleep. His mother smiled at the young man who charmed her son with his soft touch.

"I see Joseph has taken a fancy to you."

Alfie blushed as he looked down at the face of the boy sleeping in his arms.

Arthur excused himself and went off to his room. He lay across his bed after swallowing three or four aspirins. His head would not let go of the pain it had held for days. It pounded like the thumping of Joseph's drum. He glanced out his window towards the path.

"He would have died anyway, even if I would have gone for help." He spoke to himself. "If he had lived, he would have told Mama about the boys I invited to the window. She may have believed I was no better than him. I didn't plan to kill him but he made me so mad."

A few tracks remained in the light snow. From out behind a patch of alders an old stray dog strolled, its snout to the ground, testing the depth of the snow. The dog stopped at the exact spot that Arthur had met face to face with his father a few days ago.

It was white with a mangy tail. Its ears folded down like two wet leaves. The dog had a slight limp, perhaps a splinter or piece of ice caught in its paw. Arthur could not remember seeing the dog around here before. He had never seen it at the lake. What was it doing here now?

For a minute Arthur was relieved that it was not a cat. He hardly needed a black cat, with its bad luck, crossing the threshold of his misery. It was bad enough that his old man had said he was possessed by the eyes of a corpse, the eyes of the mother he hated. And that was Arthur's inheritance—the hatred Duncan felt for his mother he passed on to Arthur, and all because of his beautiful eyes.

Back in his room, he lay down on his bed and thought about the dog. Alfie didn't own a dog. He had seen plenty of hunters on his way to the lake, but none ever had a dog with them. When he woke up, it was dark. He heard his grandmother singing softly in the kitchen to Joseph. It was an old Welsh ballad about a dog; his mother had sung to him and Anntell when they were children.

When he went back to the kitchen, Anntell had her face burrowed in fiction and everyone else had left. His grandmother had gone to bed. His mother and Joseph were in her bedroom. The room swelled from the heat of the open hearth. Arthur made himself a pot of tea. His headache had gone further to the back of his head as though someone were pushing his head forward.

He looked over at Anntell who was sitting at the table.

"Have you ever seen a white dog with a mangy tail around here?"

"No, and I don't plan on searching one out."

"I saw a dog at the mouth of the path leading to the lake before I fell asleep."

"Arthur, I would be more interested if you saw a white gorilla; stop interrupting me."

"What time did Alfie leave?"

Anntell threw her book down on the table.

"I don't know; I wasn't watching the damn clock. People were in and out of here all afternoon."

"I'll bet you were your most pleasant self, Anntell."

"I know they came to get a look at Joseph. They

stared at him in awe, the bastards. Alfie's mother was the first one at the door. She came loaded down with food, two platters of it, if I'm not mistaken. What a nut bar."

"Was Alfie here?"

"He knew she would make her way to the door like Betty Crocker, so he left before her arrival. I told Mother she should put a quarantine sign on the door, but she was too polite. I would have put a 'dangerous explosive zone' sign up if it were me."

"That sign's been on this door for years; hadn't you noticed?"

"Weren't you paying attention in church? Let the dead rest."

"Rest where? Here, in Rocky Point?"

"How do I know, Arthur? I've never paid much attention to this *afterlife* business."

"Neither had I until the old man told me I had his mother's eyes. He claimed they rose from her grave and settled in my skull to haunt him."

"For the love of Jesus, Arthur, you sound like Alfred Hitchcock. That's rubbish; the man had to be crazy."

"He told me once that he hated her, that she took his father from him."

"That wouldn't surprise me. Ask Mother about her, she took care of her for quite a while."

"Ask me what?" Their mother appeared in the kitchen. Her face had a warm glow. Even her limp appeared lighter as she crossed the kitchen. Rosie Briar's face was calm, its heaviness eased.

"You knew the old man's mother. What was she really like? Arthur said father hated her," Anntell offered up like a bad cold.

Rosie Briar looked at her two older children. They looked so innocent and rather bewildered and, as she had to admit to herself, troubled.

"She was old when I tended to her; I tolerated her. I had my mother and myself to support."

"Do I have her eyes? The old man said I have her eyes."

Rosie Briar had to careful. She could see the pain on Arthur's face, the agony it had cost him. Duncan had always used a malicious tone when he spoke about Rowena to Arthur. How vicious could a person be toward his own flesh and blood?

"No, you don't, Arthur. You look like my Uncle Joe. I've known that since you were a small boy. If he thought you had her eyes, it was his mother he resented. It had nothing to do with you."

She did not look at him when she addressed his question. Arthur watched his mother through his grandmother's eyes as she made her way into the pantry. He knew by the way she had avoided his gaze, by the way her head stayed low, that she was not going to admit the truth in what his father had said.

Arthur left the kitchen and went back to his room

before his mother returned from the pantry. The heat from the hearth clung to his limbs. He felt that the cinders were under his collar and his armpits, singeing his spine. Outside his window, a cold moon outlined his father's car parked beside the garage. His mother had probably forgotten to ask someone to put it inside the garage for now.

He knew he would get to drive now that his old man was gone. His mother would pay for his lessons. He'd be free to travel wherever he pleased. A sudden bolt of freedom roared in his stomach. So what if he had the old hag's eyes. At seventeen, he could see what the future could do for him. They were both gone. He would take pleasure in tooting the horn every time he passed the graveyard.

Something was different, there, under the light of the cold moon. Something moved. It wasn't stationary like the car. It moved slowly. And sniffed. A dog moved determinedly as though following a map. The white dog was still outside—it shook its head after inspecting the tires, turned and looked straight up at Arthur standing in his window before it disappeared.

The sense of freedom soured in Arthur's stomach; he barely made it to the bathroom before he brought up violently. He wiped his mouth and made his way down the hall to the front door. He didn't feel the cool air through his shirt as he walked over to the car. Its shiny silhouette stood like a marooned iceberg in the driveway; he circled it looking for the dog. The night was silent. Through the kitchen window, he could see a glow from the fire in the hearth where his mother and Anntell were drinking tea. The dog was nowhere in sight. He walked around the garage, and up and down the lane to the road. He walked to the back door and stood on the veranda—one last look before he went into the house. A crackling in the brush, towards the path that led to the lake. The dog stood defiantly at the path's entrance, as still as a boulder. Arthur jumped the railing and headed towards the path, running towards the dog. He was breathless when he reached the mouth of the path and the emptiness that surrounded it. He walked slowly back to the veranda and opened the door quietly and went to his room. He lay under the covers without undressing. His teeth rattling, until finally he slept.

"Why didn't you tell Arthur that he is the spitting image of the old man's mother?" Anntell quizzed her mother.

"Your father always used their resemblance against him. I want to spare his feelings. Rowena Briar was quite a handsome woman. And your brother is quite handsome. His eyes are much kinder than hers could ever be. "

"Arthur didn't believe a word you said to him. The old man is gone now, Mother. You have to stop treating us the way you treat Joseph."

"I want to let him get to know himself as himself. I won't have him believing he is just a remnant of Rowena Briar."

"She must have been a miserable old sow."

"She was a very angry woman. Nothing ever pleased her: her marriage fell apart; her husband drank himself into a stupor. She controlled everything in sight."

"I would have dropped her into an open well, Mother."

"That wasn't really an option, dear. I married your father when I was barely thirty. The future saw me before I saw it. Where could I lead my blind mother? I couldn't leave her on her own. My choices were limited."

"I'm not blaming you, Mother."

"Had I known what happened in that family, I would never have gone to work for Rowena Briar. My mother tried to warn me that all was not well between those walls. My cousin wanted us to move west, but your grandmother didn't want to leave Rocky Point. She wanted to be close to my father's grave. She said we'd manage, somehow. And I wasn't about to accept public welfare; I had my own pride, still do in a way. I wasn't going to let my disability stop me."

Rosie had given her daughter all the information she ever would about that time with Rowena Briar. She was not about to reveal what their grandmother had said on her deathbed. There was no reason for Anntell and Arthur to know what had caused their grandfather Charlie Briar's death. What good would that information do them? They hadn't even known the man.

Perhaps she should have mentioned to Duncan what his mother had revealed to her. Would it have dissolved some of his anger? She was aware of the scorn he felt for his mother. For most women, except for Anntell. She looked too much like Charlie Briar for him to unravel her; she was his last link to whatever twisted love he had left. No doubt, as a child, he had been capable of giving and receiving real love from his father. And then it had stopped. Cold as a winter stone.

11

ROSIE CHECKED IN on Arthur before she went to bed. What had distracted him to the point that he left the kitchen before she returned from the pantry? Anntell was right; he did not believe a word she had told him about Duncan's mother. She pulled down the blanket and rustled his hair. She was surprised to see him fully dressed with his head huddled under a blanket. Why was he still in his street clothes under the covers? His face looked tired and drawn for lack of sleep in days. The suddenness of his father's death must have caught up with him; the crowds that surrounded him, the people whose eyes sought out Joseph as if the poor child himself was a corpse. Their lives had been exposed through something that should have been private. It was a mockery to Duncan to have people look into his waxy face, examine the depth of the scowl on his brow, the fury running under his skin like water under thin ice. He was an angry corpse and most people were aware of it.

Arthur opened his eyes and saw the deep love in his mother's eyes, the love she had been forced to keep silent for so long. For a brief moment he felt his life had begun anew; he had his mother's and grandmother's unconditional love. Yes, his father had a part in his own demise, and perhaps Arthur had done his family a favour by letting the man that shadowed their lives die. Arthur had made it possible for Joseph to view life beyond his bedroom window.

It did not seem to concern his mother that everyone knew the Briars had three children. She smiled on each new day. People came to the house to visit. Rosie Briar had set up an appointment in Halifax with a specialist for Joseph. She was free to come and go as she pleased. Arthur could speak to his mother of his fears and what cavities his father's death had created in him now. He could tell her it wasn't Joseph he wanted to expose, but the fear and pain of living with his father. She would understand; he assured himself.

But he was wrong. After his mother left his room, new fears tore into his head at a tremendous speed. He paced the room in circles. The house was quiet and dark. A cave of agony in what should have been relief. He made his way to the kitchen and watched the last of the dying embers in the hearth. They huddled together like a pack of fireflies twinkling themselves to death until nothing but a small mound of ashes lay upon the grate.

Arthur made himself a strong cup of tea and sat at the kitchen table. A slice of moonlight wedged itself between the branches of a tall pine tree near the window. The branches rotated in slow motion against the night. A clean procession of snowflakes released themselves, swirling through the air and to the ground. Why had he not paid attention to such beauty before? Wind crooned in the eaves. A melodic arrangement for violins and the harp, thought Arthur. Nature had never caught his attention in this manner. He trampled through flowers as a mountain climber, threw rocks at the sea, carved graffiti in the sand. He walked through nature, inhaled wind in his lungs, and yet he had taken for granted that he owed nature the privileges of its wonders. At the lake, he sought only silence.

He had finished his tea when he noticed movement below the window. A shadow sniffed at the falling snowflakes and moved awkwardly, searching for a spot to lay low. Arthur stood up and watched its movement. The dog reared its head and backed up towards the tree as it kept its eyes on him. The cup fell from Arthur's hand and crashed under the table. He moved quickly to the porch door and out around the side of the house below the kitchen window. He was too close; the dog couldn't get out of his sight this time. Beside the tall pine, the snowflakes continued to swirl. They moved around his still figure and landed at his feet. There were no signs of the dog.

Arthur cleaned up the pieces of the broken cup and made his way back to bed. He did not bother to check his window. The dog was the least of his worries, he told himself, as he shivered under his quilt. It was voiceless, unlike the boys he had brought to Joseph's window. How long would it be before his mother or Anntell would hear about his escapades? It was his mother he was worried about most. The whole village knew about Joseph since his father's death. He could see the judgment of his mother in people's eyes when they came to the house.

"Why would she have stayed with such a cruel man?" He imagined them thinking, "The money no doubt."

"Was she as responsible as that man for keeping that poor child a secret?"

"How could a woman deny her own flesh and blood?"

He knew what was being talked about in the stores and the post office of Rocky Point. What was to stop the boys from throwing their two cents' worth into the fray, now that there was no attraction at the geranium window? This would be something else to add to the family's woes. His father was dead, and yet there would still be no peace for Arthur if this news got out. Could he tell his mother that he had brought the boys to see Joseph to get even with his father? He would break her heart. He could never ask her to forgive him for such cruelty. She would never have expected Arthur to betray her or to exploit Joseph. She would think he was as cold as their father had been to her beloved child.

He was losing control. He deliberately avoided the boys he had brought to the window. He avoided going into town if at all possible. He was happy he didn't have to go to church. But how long would it be before his mother would begin to question his behaviour? She would know it wasn't grief. He had to speak with someone. Alfie Johns knew what he had done; he had confronted him three years ago about what he had heard in the schoolyard. It was a sure bet that Alfie would never tell his mother. He was too solid a person to be mean to her. He liked Joseph and respected his family, and was crazy about his sister, Arthur reasoned. He would speak to Alfie.

Arthur Briar stammered his confession into the deep blue sea rather than into the quiet, observant face of Alfie Johns. They had met by coincidence near the shore where Alfie photographed seagulls on a slice of drift ice. It was early spring. The wind chimed from the northwest and carried Arthur's confession into the waves and back again with a heavy thud.

"This...w-white...dog...keeps a...ppearing and...and dis...disappearing in...in front of... me," he stammered.

Alfie watched Arthur's face cringe painfully at each broken vowel.

"Do you know why?" Alfie asked quietly.

"It's...a ghost...a ghost plays t-tricks on people."

"Why do you believe it's a ghost, Arthur?"

"I k-k-killed him."

"Who did you kill?"

"Him...m-my father."

"How did you kill your father?" Alfie Johns realized he was speaking to someone at his breaking point. He had to be delicate with him and get him help as soon as possible.

"He was...was mad at me. He...heard the k-k-kids... talking at the store. He...knew I took them...to see Jo...seph at the window. He was...furious. He called me names. I swore...swore... back at him. And then he felt...pain in his chest and...and...fell. He died... on the ground. And I...just stood... and...watched, and then...then...went on to the lake."

Arthur was cold and broken as Alfie Johns put his arm around him to calm him.

"You didn't kill anyone, Arthur. Your father would have died from his heart condition sooner or later. I don't know if help had arrived if he would have survived, and neither do you."

"No...no, no. I k-k-killed...him. I wanted...wanted him...to die...I wanted...him...to die ...for...a long... time ."

"Arthur, you need to talk to someone ."

"My mother...will be mad that I brought those...kids

to see Jo...seph. Sh-she'll hate me too. I wanted them to...to see how mean my fa-fa...ther could be to us. He hated... me...I'm possessed with...with his mother's eyes...h-he said...that to me. "

"I understand your worry, Arthur. Why don't you speak to your mother? She knows how unfairly you were treated. She'll understand. I can listen and offer her my support, but you need someone who can help you."

Arthur's body stiffened. His head turned towards the breakwater as his frightened eyes followed something in motion.

"There! Do you...see it? The white...dog."

"There's nothing over there, Arthur; take it easy. There's not a soul on the breakwater. Not a person or an animal. I want to help you. Why don't I speak to your mother for you?"

He turned his attention back to Alfie, and stood now with his fists in the air. His voice stammered in long gasps.

"Li-ar, li-ar. Li-ar. You will...will make my...mother hate me. I tried to...to ca-catch that dog and...and make...its heart...stop...beating. "

Arthur plunged his fist into Alfie's stomach, violently and hard. Alfie had not seen it coming; he hit the sand on his back. Arthur's eyes a fever, burning raw. His hair was greasy and unruly. His teeth filmed over. His speech almost incoherent as he shouted at the invisible white dog on the breakwater.

"Go...go...go to hell, dog...burn in hell!"

Alfie reached out, after a few minutes, to pull his camera bag towards him. He scrambled to his feet and watched Arthur Briar stride towards his home. Alfie had two choices to consider carefully as he stumbled in the sand: to go and reveal the agonies and danger of a seventeen year old on the edge to someone in authority, or to inform Rosie Briar of the help her son required, because of an invisible white dog whose heart refused to stop beating.

He'd wait it out a couple of days and speak to Anntell first; together they could speak to her mother. It would be better to let the family handle the situation.

12

ROSIE BRIAR TUCKED Joseph under his warm quilt before she settled into her own bed. She smiled as she rubbed his forehead. She had bought a new bed for Joseph and had it set up in her room. She pulled the quilt up to her chin and turned out the lamp. This is where she did her best thinking. Her best resolutions came out of the dark. Except one, she thinks, remembering back to June of 1943 when she married Duncan Briar against her mother's advice.

"He is a bully, you'll have a life of torment and regret with that man. Women are objects to him. I always judge a man by the way he treats his mother," Isla Jones informed her daughter.

Rosie knew that Duncan Briar was quick tempered with the rest of the staff. She always tried to be out of the house before he came home from work. On several occasions he had come home early to be around her; he had never tried to abuse her in any way. She was frightened for her job if he were dissatisfied with her work. She was paid much more than anyone else. This, along with the small income from her cousin, made life comfortable for her and her mother. Where else could she make such a high salary? She was not trained for anything else. Nursing and teaching were out of the question because of her foot.

"I hope she didn't give you much trouble today, my dear."

Duncan stood by her side as she folded his mother's clothing. Her hand trembled around the satin slips and expensive underwear she folded as slim as napkins. She had it down to a pattern. What went where, and in what order.

She noticed a small smile warm his face as he held up a slip. He imagined Rosie in such exquisite wear, the satin clinging to her white skin, folding into creases a hand would envy. He had to be careful not to scare her away. She would, one day, be his. He amused himself with the thought of Rosie Jones between the creases of the Briar sheets. But he would have to wait longer than he anticipated. Rowena Briar lived on defiantly another ten years.

"I know you are waiting for me to go." Her raspy voice clawed at Duncan's nerves like a pesky cat.

Duncan Briar knotted his fists. "You're a crazy old nuisance, woman. You ruined my father's life, and now you believe I'm next in your line of fire."

"There is no doubt I'll succeed. I've seen the way you

look at Rosie; she's too good for you. I've learned that over the years. She's not one of those tramps you keep on the side. You're a coward, just like your father. Men like you don't love women, they just torment them."

"That's what you think, but you won't live to see the day she'll become my wife."

Rowena died a week later, on Duncan's forty-ninth birthday, with a smile on her face. He proposed to Rosie right after the funeral. He sounded like a salesmen: she would have wealth and a beautiful home and two businesses for her needs and comfort for life; her mother would be taken care of and could move into the Briar house; he would keep the help on a weekly basis to do the heavy cleaning.

Rosie Jones weighed the options for romance and a fiancé in her life for a short time. At thirty, a high-school dropout with a lame foot, she was not in great demand. She had known Duncan long enough, she thought, and had learned to put up with his eccentric ways.

It was a small wedding. She wore a cream-coloured suit and a deep salmon-coloured corsage of roses on her right lapel. Her shoes were creamed-coloured, a coincidence she remembers. She had ordered white from the catalogue, but they were unavailable so the store had sent along, with an apology, a more expensive pair of shoes in cream. They matched her suit perfectly.

She and Duncan were married by a justice of the peace in a building that was being renovated; Rosie remembers having to walk through sawdust and around lumber to get to the office. Their two witnesses: her friend, June, and one of Duncan's employees. The justice of the peace was a small man with a pointed goatee. He peered over his rimless glasses and looked directly into her eyes. Specks of sawdust coated the elbows of his black suit jacket.

"How old are you, young lady?" He spoke directly to Rosie, an air of concern in his voice.

"Thirty, sir."

He adjusted his glasses and proceeded with an air of doubt. She had a very youthful look, plagued by innocence.

Rosie could feel Duncan's muscles stiffen by her side. He seemed ready to address the man crudely, but remained silent throughout the five-minute ceremony. Afterwards they went back to the Briar home where the cook had prepared a roast dinner and a cake, one, Rosie believed, to fill in for a wedding cake. It had something ornate on top, but she cannot remember what exactly. It resembled a pistol. The witnesses ate hurriedly and left shortly afterward.

Duncan suggested they go for a drive along the scenic route of Rocky Point and stop later to watch the sunset near the foot of the mountain. Before they left, he advised his bride to change into more casual clothing for the long ride. Rosie had brought a small case with her personal wear and a shift of clothes before she left her mother's house. Her neighbour, Charlotte, was staying with her mother until the next day when she'd move into the Briar house. Rosie had packed a green cotton dress and a pink nightdress before she left. She was taking them out of the case when Duncan came into the room and locked the door behind him.

"I'll be ready in a jiffy," said Rosie without turning to look at her new husband.

"I hope so," he replied. "I'll help you out of your suit."

"I can manage." He stood beside her and sat her down on the bed.

"I gave the cook the rest of the day off." His tone was anxious, almost urgent. "Do you know how long you've kept me waiting for this?"

She stared up at him. Panic set her lame foot to twitch uncontrollably.

He began to remove her suit, first her jacket and then her blouse. He moved his hand behind her back and unclipped her bra. He ordered her to stand and removed her skirt and slip, then tore at her underwear.

"Walk towards the door and back to the bed!"

Rosie could feel her muscles weaken. Her foot ached so badly she had to grip the door handle for support. When she turned Duncan was under the sheet and leaning up against the pillows. His shirt and suit were slung over a chair. He examined her lean body as she approached the bed. Her lame leg slightly shorter than the other.

"Get under the sheets, Rosie!"

She stumbled her way back to the bed and nervously slid in beside him. She watched the fan above her head move in slow motion. It was shaped like large leaves from a palm tree. She had never been in this room before. It was kept locked at all times. Green and gold wallpaper covered the walls; it had an intricate pattern: women in long gowns fanning themselves in majestic gazebos as large white swans swam by on ponds. The ceilings were over twelve feet in height; heavy green velvet drapes made the room dark and cool. Outside the window, Rosie could hear the cry of an eagle.

Duncan pulled the sheet from her body as she lay, terrified, beside him. This angered him. Frightened women made poor lovers. His hand moved swiftly over her body, stopping to pleat her nipples between his heavy fingers; he laughed when she pleaded with him to stop. He grabbed her lame foot and massaged the tremble in her bones. Her moans of agony were answered in a way she never understood. She had imagined it all wrong, the tenderness, the gentle lover, the comfort for life, the champagne and roses. The "I love you forever" promises.

She watched the fan above her head swirl round and round. She felt the weight of his body over her, a desire to take a deep breath to keep from smothering, the deep penetration that sliced into her like a blade. When she came to, she was alone in the bed. She leaned up against the pillow and pulled back the sheet. He had changed the bed, dressed her in her nightdress and tied back her hair with a pink ribbon.

He returned to the room with a silver tea tray and two cups of tea. Rosie could not look into his eyes as he sat down on the bed and offered her a cup.

"Here, Mrs. Briar, I know you like your tea hot and strong."

The cup rattled on the saucer as she sipped slowly from the hot brew. She desperately wanted to get up and go home. She could feel his eyes on her every move. He laughed as she struggled with the cup and saucer.

"I've changed my mind about our scenic tour, Rosie; I don't think you are up to a long drive."

She could hear the anger in his voice when she refused to answer him. He pulled the cup and saucer from her hands and placed them roughly on the side table, then turned her face towards him.

"Look at me when I speak to you!"

Rosie lifted her eyes slowly and looked at Duncan Briar. She hoped that she could conceal her hatred from him.

"I've had many women in my day, dear wife, and they all loved what I had to offer. In time you will love it, too."

"Thank you for the tea, Duncan. It was good." She mumbled in a child's voice.

He grabbed her arm and tightened his grip on her wrist.

"Do you honestly believe I was talking about tea?"

He let go of her wrist and moved his hand under her nightdress between her legs.

"You are going to need more training than I expected, Mrs. Briar."

He had a strong jaw that twitched as he spoke. His lips were full and wide, and when he finished speaking he'd sink his teeth into his bottom lip, punctuating the importance of each statement he made. Rosie watched his teeth sink deep into his lip. She knew what he was thinking by his physical actions alone. She had known him long enough to know what he planned, he'd execute. He climbed back into bed and pulled the sheet over them. She watched the blades of the fan scatter the warm air of the room and send down a soft breeze along her brow as her husband sank his teeth into her breast.

When it was over, he made her go to the kitchen and bring back the tray. She flushed her face in cold water in the pantry sink to clear her head. What would he do if she made her escape? He would know where to find her. She was afraid for her mother's safety; her mother would be left in peril should he force her to move away. She had made her bed, and from this day forward, would have to lie in it with Duncan Briar more times than she cared.

Rosie heard Joseph stir in his sleep. She fumbled out of bed to see to him. She was happy for the distraction. She lifted Joseph in her arms and rocked him in the rocking chair beside his bed. He reached up to touch her face. His small hand was warm. A kiss on the cheek warm. How gentle he was; a real little gentleman, her Joseph, a charmer.

"Mama is here, Joseph; Mama is here."

Rosie could feel his body relaxing in her arms as she held him. A flame of anger welled in her chest. She took quick short breaths to quench the flame. She could not have her child sense her feelings about a man who would never again enter their lives, a man who had never entered Joseph's life without contempt.

She was tormented by Arthur's behaviour. And what were Anntell's plans? Anntell was free to go as she pleased, now that she had graduated. Something crawled back into her head, something that she has not wanted to deal with for so long. Something for which she felt very responsible, as any mother should. The demise of her own children concerned her. She could already see it happening to Arthur. He was coming apart piece by piece, a frail wanderer under a midnight storm, in tatters. She had drowned out the name of Joseph's condition years ago when she and her friend, Charlotte, sneaked him to a doctor to have him checked every six months. She remembers mumbling the word the doctor used, but had never repeated it again—there was no cure for it anyway.

She still remembers the man's round face when he spoke to her. He was kind, but professionally assertive, a stance doctors take when death has the upper hand.

"Your child will not live beyond his late teens or early twenties, Mrs. Briar."

She welcomed the comfort of her bed after putting Joseph back to sleep. The room was freshly aired. She had chosen her favourite colour for the walls to be painted in the spring. A periwinkle blue. She had read somewhere that blue has a calming effect on people. She needed that peace for herself. She had earned it. It would be good for Joseph to be surrounded by peace when the time came. She whispered the words quietly to herself.

"He will be fifteen soon. If only a coat of paint could affect the lives of my other children."

Rosie made plans in her head, the ones she regrets not making when Duncan was still living. What could he have done that hadn't already happened? She would get help for Arthur, the help he had needed for so many years. It was obvious to her how his behaviour had changed since his father's death. He was on edge, panicky, withdrawn. What was he afraid of, now that his father was gone? She would approach him gently. She would have the boss at the mill teach him the ropes. He could have a good job there if he desired, once he felt better. He was smart and strong, if only Duncan had taken the time to notice.

Anntell was different. She would get away from here as soon as she could. She had seen as much of Rocky Point as she wanted to see. Rosie was surprised she had stayed on this long, longer than anyone expected.

She was happy for the time she had with Joseph, whose health was, at the moment, not in any grave danger. And her mother was healthy despite her vision loss. She would make sure Isla would be guided freely around this house.

13

ARTHUR SNUCK BACK home and sat behind the garage where he couldn't be seen. He checked his pockets again to make sure he hadn't forgotten the car keys. If Alfie Johns could keep his mouth shut, Arthur could proceed with his plans for one ride. He had heard his mother on the phone with someone who was interested in buying his old man's car. He would not want to see it go without his wish fulfilled; he had always dreamt of sitting behind the wheel of the black coupe.

The front of the coupe was facing the lane; someone must have taken it for a test drive, Arthur assumed. Good; he wouldn't have to back the damn thing out when he left. He spoke to himself in a clear voice. It didn't matter to him that he didn't have a license. He would take the back road leading up to the mountain. He would stop at the store at the foot of the mountain and get a cold drink. How would they know if he had a license? You didn't need a license to buy a damn bottle of pop. He was free of his father's commands and insults. He would not have to worry about the stress on his dear mother.

He knew how to drive a damn car as well as the next guy. He and a couple of boys had driven an old truck through a field several times when they were younger, and he was the best driver amongst them. How hard could the car be once you got it moving? He wouldn't go all the way over the mountain. There were lots of turn-offs where he could turn around and head back. His mother would be angry, but he would convince her to let him get a license and his own car. At his age, there was no reason he couldn't own a car. And they could certainly afford one.

Arthur kept his eye on the lane and watched out for Alfie Johns. He would stop Alfie from entering the house. He'd bust that fucking camera of his if he protested. But what if he phoned? No, Alfie was an in-your-face kind of guy, a talker. He'd want to face his mother with that sympathetic voice of his, like an undertaker's. Arthur swore and spit on the ground to clear his throat. Why did he have to blab to Alfie anyway? Alfie liked the family, but he might also intervene, to make himself look important in Anntell's eyes. How would he know Arthur needed help? He probably would have hated the old man himself. And now he thinks *help* is required. He believes there was no fucking dog on the breakwater. He's the crazy one: the dog was looking right at him.

Arthur was relieved that nobody came near the house. Alfie would think things over, the fool. It's funny he didn't try and get a picture of the make-believe dog. Arthur should have nailed him harder for saying he didn't see it. There is no way he could have missed that white dog on the breakwater. Arthur could hear the sound of his own heart racing at the sight of that dog on the breakwater, its mangy tail scraping the planks, its strong back in attack mode. This time he had seen its snarling teeth, its pointed fangs.

The sun would be setting soon. Arthur felt his stomach growl with hunger from the aroma of a pork roast whiffing out from under the pantry window. He remembers his mother talking about a chocolate cake with boiled frosting for dessert. She always made him a chocolate cake for his birthday with extra frosting. Perhaps there was some way he could sneak in after everyone left the kitchen. She would have put a plate aside for him to warm up.

He stood up, stretched, and relieved himself against a tree. Two blue jays fought over something at the corner of the garage. They were nasty birds, always pecking away at something wherever they landed. One soared upward towards the eave of the house with something between its beak. Arthur did not see where the loser had gone. "To each his own," he mumbled under his breath. He wasn't going to lose this opportunity.

Arthur remembered what his father said to him once, something about his mother taking his father from him. She must have trained him well when she got him. He took what he wanted and lost. Arthur kept an eye on the kitchen window. A shadow appeared between a crack in the pantry blind, no doubt his mother watching out to see if he were walking up the lane. He heard the slamming of the porch door as Anntell came out and made her way slowly down the lane. She was probably on her way to the library or to meet up with Alfie somewhere.

Arthur wasn't concerned; he'd be gone before she came back home. His mother would be at the back of the house with Joseph, getting him settled for the night. His poor grandmother would think a car had driven into the yard when she heard the roar of the engine and the slamming of a car door. His getaway was easier than he anticipated. He felt the key in his pocket. He'd wait to make sure Anntell was well on her way before he made his way down the long lane.

Arthur wedged his way behind the wheel and sank slowly into the plush red seat. He felt the smooth steering wheel as though he were stroking a circle of ivory in his hands. He checked out the silver lighter and pulled a cigarette from his shirt pocket. This was probably how James Dean felt behind the wheel. This was even more than he had imagined. It was not something his old man would allow. He turned the ignition slowly, and the engine purred with the passion of its own power. The gas tank registered full. The dashboard lit up like the cockpit of a jet. He pressed lightly on the gas pedal and jutted away from the Briar house. An eloquent thief in the falling night. After a few minutes the car's engine smoothed into a rhythmic pattern.

Arthur turned right at the end of the lane and moved on towards the back road that led to the foot of the mountain. He had not met any traffic so far. There were no other cars at the store, but he decided not to take a chance and go in. There could be too many questions to answer. He noticed a red light flashing on the dash, but he couldn't take his eyes off the road to check anything out. The damn thing was blinking like a Christmas tree.

The flashing began to aggravate him as he crept along. He could see the sign for the mountain road up ahead. He pressed down hard on the accelerator and the car lunged ahead as if someone had pushed him forward several feet from behind. He had not anticipated the car's power. Tread lightly, he cautioned himself. Tread lightly. The light continued to flash. He came to a stop and checked it out. "Check Oil" flashed off and on. To hell with the oil. He wasn't going far enough to burn much oil. If he killed the engine, who would know? He'd be back before anyone noticed the car was gone.

Arthur could see the incline of the mountain a few

feet in front of him. It stretched out sleek and dark. The back of a black panther. This image made him smile. This is what he wanted, the thrill of the climb, his ability to succeed without anyone's directions or insults. Who could stop him now? He moved on. He opened the windows to let in the wind. The black coupe purred. He got a quick glance of the sharp embankments on both sides of him along the edge of the road.

He watched for a turn-off as the car climbed further up the mountain. He saw a sign to his left and pulled in slowly. A cold sweat leaked down his back; he had climbed further than he'd planned. He smoked a cigarette, then backed up and turned down the mountain.

He had only gone a few feet when he noticed the shadow in the middle of the road. The slamming of the brakes caused a haunting, howling sound. The smell of burning rubber filled the car. Arthur watched the shadow as it moved closer to him.

His body trembled as the white dog became visible in the bright headlights. He closed the windows quickly. There was no way he could miss hitting the dog now; he'd finally get rid of it and nobody would ever know. He pressed down on the accelerator. The black coupe, in high gear, slid from side to side. There was no one there, no one to tell Arthur Briar to shift the coupe into low gear, to slow down for the sharp turn ahead, to tap the breaks lightly on his descent, or that what he believed he saw was only a figment of his imagination. Arthur clung desperately to the wheel as he hit the gravel and the car flew down over the cliff.

The black coupe plunged into the sea as the dog rose above the water like pure, white mist.

14

ROSIE BRIAR BURIED her son on a Friday, almost eighteen years to the day he was born. She felt the deep peace of Fridays, when her husband would journey off somewhere to restock supplies or visit museums, or whatever it was that Duncan Briar did to gather sensation in his life. Duncan had also been buried on a Friday, but this left no sentiment in Rosie's mind.

She stood by Arthur's grave after ushering the others back to the house. She watched as Anntell and Alfie got into the funeral car and drove out of the cemetery with the driver. Anntell begged her mother to come back with them. She felt uneasy leaving her beside what remained of Arthur's body when he was pulled from the Atlantic and an open hole in the ground.

"There is something I have to see to before I go back home," Rosie Briar insisted.

The gravediggers huddled together for a smoke and spoke in hushed tones, keeping an eye on her through their blue cigarette smoke. They were not sure of her state of mind, as they whispered behind their nicotine-and-mud-caked fingers. In all their years of burying the dead, they had acquired the means of detecting outbursts of grief from madness. They knew the signs, these rugged men who had the task of tucking loved ones in for the last time. Manic screams and attempts to throw oneself into the open grave were few.

What they saw a few feet away from them was a lovely woman in a dark blue dress and coat. She wore brown pumps. A brown shawl draped part of her head and shoulders. She stood looking down at the casket laid in the grave. The family wreath made up of wildflowers lay close to her feet. She stood, erect with the dignity of a woman in controlled mourning. She had come to bury her son, to offer him the most heart-wrenching gesture any mother could give her child: her ability to place him back into the womb of Mother Earth.

She turned quietly and asked the men if she had time to place the wildflowers from the wreath in Arthur's grave. One by one she sorted the wildflowers and dropped them down over his casket. She had chosen her favourites and Arthur's: tiger lilies, daisies, buttercups and lupines. In her too-quiet grief (people noticed she never shed a tear), she had reached out for something to lighten her darkness, an underground rainbow for Arthur.

Anntell returned and was at her side when the last shovels of clay were spread over Arthur's grave. She took her mother's arm as they walked along the cemetery road to the waiting taxi. Rosie Briar turned her head and watched the three men resting their arms on their shovels. From a distance, they resembled shepherds upon a hill, waiting and watching. She walked quietly amongst the dead: the long-ago dead now in someone's memory as insignificant as dust swirling into an open door, and removed without too much fuss; the not-too-long-ago dead still mourned, remembered for something as mischievous as a practical joke. Their legacy alive in epitaphs chiseled in marble stones:

Lived to laugh—Laughed to live

In the Briar cemetery plot, no secrets are revealed in death. Charlie Briar rests under his name only. Rowena Stewart Briar returned to dust under a subtle farewell: *At Last*.

Rosie Briar has not had a headstone erected for her husband. She would have to wait until the ground had settled, she was informed. She had not paid much attention to the grave at all. When the time came, date of birth and death would be sufficient: Duncan Briar had already offered his epitaph to the living.

15

IT WASN'T UNTIL after Arthur's death that Alfie revealed to Anntell his meeting with her brother down at the shore.

"He was in bad shape when I last saw him. I had every intention of telling you, thinking then we could speak to your mother together."

Anntell looked around as though she had been asked a question and was searching out the voice rolling in on a wave. Who was speaking in this vacuum between life and death about her brother? About the wounds that festered for so long you believe you can heal them by watching your father die. Arthur and her father. Her father and Arthur. But this conversation between them is not silent. Arthur's voice is raging. Fighting back. He is a mad dog on the last thread of his shattered leash. And his father is in the way. Has always been in the way.

"Poor Arthur. He beat us to it, didn't he, Alfie?" She eyed him with a vacant look. "My mother planned on getting him help. She knew something went wrong for Arthur a long time ago."

Her mother had known from the day she married Duncan Briar that something, that *everything*, was wrong.

"Without a doubt, Arthur would have found a way to confuse anyone who tried to help him. We lived under the same roof for eighteen years. I know what he thought, Alfie.

"*Multiple choice, Arthur, you can't get them wrong. It's your life in A, B, or C,*" Anntell said, imagining how a psychiatrist might have hopelessly approached her brother. "Arthur would have stayed on the sidelines and watched the help try and put him back together, flake by flake, with a grin on his face. Anger and rage have a long arm and a short smile. He would have smiled between the questions: *How was the relationship between your parents? Do you believe he ever loved your mother?*

"Arthur would have spit out his answer, Alfie. All dying men have a confession to make. They believe it's required for redemption. I can't remember everything the old man said.

"This would have disturbed him, the idea of having our father talk about loving anyone. Arthur mentioned to me once how he liked to watch mother dance around the dining-room floor. I never saw this myself. But he would have seen this as something she performed for him only, to let him know that she had her happy moments. He would have made his answer quite clear to anyone trying to help him.

"*I wanted my mother left alone. I wanted to watch her dance by herself, without interruptions; each muscle in her beautiful, pale legs stretching out their freedom on the dining-room floor. He never bothered her while she danced, because it only happened when he was out of the house. I dreaded the thoughts of my mother dancing with my father.*

"*Do you believe your father had his own issues with his parents?* Arthur would not be tricked by this game of tag, Alfie. He would have belted his answer out.

"Destroy your children and they will destroy their own. Tag. Tag. Bull. Easy enough to pass the buck when someone is broken. A bull in the morning is still a fucking bull at night. Look what he did to Joseph. He made him invisible. What he couldn't make disappear, he broke.

"*All the king's horses and all the king's men couldn't put Duncan Briar together again*. My father broke him and left him in pieces."

Anntell's words would have been softer for her mother's ears. Whatever her mother did to provide for a future would keep her in the past. She was the co-contributor of the three masses of eggs and the sperm she gave names to, and in her own way she tried to love and protect them equally. Arthur is gone and Joseph's frail life is on hold.

Alfie Johns' face sweats sympathy. His fierce secret tumbles out of his mouth. The messenger with his own life in his hands inhales deeply.

"He was a very angry young man, but he wasn't a killer. He just wanted to kill the pain, Anntell. He couldn't carry it any longer."

Anntell has a desire to hold him tenderly, to assure him that he had arrived too late in the Briar triangle to cause any more pain, but she remains at a distance from him. It didn't work the first time she tried to hold Alfie Johns. He unwrapped her arms from him like a gift that required special handling.

"I see no need to tell mother about him inviting the boys to the window to see Joseph. That could be very hard on her. What if she saw this act as Arthur turning into our father."

Anntell can hear the voice of a woman she has never met in her life as she directs commands to Alfie. She imagines this is how her grandmother Rowena's voice sounded, raw and greedy for battle. Anntell's voice peels back scraps of anger and disgust. She wants to feed it to somebody, to give it away to the nearest taker. Drop it over the wharf to drown out the whole fucking lot. She must soften her voice around Alfie. He is someone she does not want to puncture. He has her best interest at heart.

"I hate this place more every day," she blurted out, "I

feel I'm being held in solitary confinement with clay beneath my feet." She sighed wearily before speaking again. "Arthur came to my room looking for a cigarette. I told him he was weak, that he had to stand up to the old man. That was the day my father died."

There may have been a different outcome if she had looked out her bedroom window on that day, scraped a circle in the frost with her nails like she used to do as a child. She looked out at the world around her through a circle of frost on long winter days, brushed the frost dust away with the end of her braids. Once she had seen a fox hurry off down the path with their cat, Rob Roy, in its mouth. She and Arthur had built two or three snowmen in the back field. Their twig fingers reached out far enough to touch one another. Their grandmother knitted red scarves and hats for the snow people. The fox sneaked slowly past the cold figures with their scarves filled with wind, and left red dots of blood in the snow to the match the colour of the scarves.

Anntell knows that she could have defused the explosion near the geranium window. She could have called for help herself. All it would have taken was one circle opened in the frost to keep Arthur Briar alive. But she had her records playing full blast and heard nothing.

"You will have to tell her about Arthur meeting your father. She will understand why he did what he did. I don't think you have to mention Joseph."

Alfie Johns has chosen his words carefully. Like walking around an open grave where the ground is rough. A hidden sod here and there under the clay, and you've caved in. His face is serious. He is talking to the woman in Rocky Point that he loves. He is telling her why he believes her brother is dead. And why her father might have died, even if he'd gotten help. Love and death—deep subjects for two people just twenty years of age: a collective of forty years, coming together between two hearts stopped dead for seemingly different reasons. Alfie won't say what he believes to be true. Not at this time. He cannot say that Duncan Briar and his son both died from regret. People die every day with regret plastered on their faces. Doctors will call it stress, but that's the explanation when all the factors haven't been added up. Anntell is not only in mourning; she's also in a state of regret, the worse place for someone who has weaned herself off of fiction as reality slowly seeps in between the blanks and falls between the lines.

Alfie swallows, "Jesus Christ" in a deep breath. He knows that Anntell has inherited the regret gene of the Briars. They had never learned to communicate. They saved all their regret for the edge of their graves. Anntell has to dig deep to find her voice. Unravel her words. Alfie can hear the sea shifting into high tide. A cooling fog rises, ambushing their bodies in swirling clouds. A mob of magical spinners and weavers unleashed from the sea to catch them in their web.

Anntell begins to say something, but stops. She wants this memory to last. She wants Arthur's voice again in her head. She cannot remember if she had heard it correctly the first time Arthur crept into her room with a large smile on his face. He did not stammer his words when he told her about the girl named Irene.

"Anntell, you'll never guess what happened tonight."

"I can't say I will."

"I was down at the wharf and I met...," he hesitated and lit a cigarette.

"You met what, Arthur, a seagull?"

"Do you want to hear my fucking story or not?"

"You're going to tell me anyway."

"I met up with this girl who really likes me. Her name is Irene. We danced together lots of times at the hall. She doesn't go to our school. She stays at her cousin's some weekends."

"How often did you dance with her?

"Two or three dances, who's counting?"

"Oh, you mean it was love at first step, Arthur?"

"It was even more than that, Anntell, we did it."

Anntell closed her novel. An impish grin crossed her face.

"What? You threw rocks into the sea."

"No, we made out. It was awesome. The only thing

she complained about was the tobacco stink on my neck. She doesn't smoke."

"Good for her, she doesn't smoke. How old is Irene, dear brother?"

"My age, almost eighteen."

"Good for you, but I hope you were well protected."

"We were. The fog was so thick we couldn't see our hands in front of us."

"For fuck sakes, Arthur, the fog can't stop a girl from getting pregnant."

"Oh that, don't worry, Irene's on the pill. She has some queer trouble that happens to girls."

"Don't we all, Arthur. It's called sex. Just be cautious."

"She's going to come skating sometime with me on the lake this winter. I can't wait."

Perhaps that is how it went down. The ecstasy of a first love, or even the possibility of it, had made him smile. Did Irene even exist, or was she a phantom of desire?

Something about this conversation, this innocent confession, this man-boy who got to taste the other side of hate behind a veil of white mist, will stay with her. She hadn't even asked him what the girl looked like or what she was wearing. When were they planning on meeting again? What had Irene seen in Arthur that so many people had missed? She must have been happy for her brother. Hadn't she been?

She had listened to his story. But his story, real or

imagined, had a different outcome than hers. Life had turned out differently for her under the wharf, and she'd laughed off his confession as he spoke. Had hearing this been too hard to digest? Had it been too hard to swallow her hurt pride? How dare Arthur, clumsy Arthur, dangling like a tangled puppet in a burst of ecstasy fitting himself into a girl-woman as she swam into his youthful lust? This is a memory she will not squander, even though it could be fiction, his narrative too extravagant in relaying his secret to change the tide now and forever.

16

AT NINETEEN YEARS of age, with her father and brother lying side by side in the Briar family plot, Anntell bid farewell to part of her life. Arthur's grave was still a heap of clay—the ground hadn't settled him in as yet—when wanderlust stroked Anntell Briar's feet. She had graduated from high school. She had a healthy sum of money left to her from her father's estate. She was convinced that her life would be delayed if she inhaled one more breath of Rocky Point air into her lungs.

The Briar house became as still as an empty school yard in summer, where only the breezes and butterflies go to play. Joseph, taken out of the back room after his father's death, smiled at the faces that surrounded him daily. His grandmother held him on her lap, and scanned his slim body with her clever hands, taking notes. "What parts of him were missing?" she asked herself in silence.

Rosie Briar introduced Joseph to a new toilet seat, a child's seat covered with colourful birds swaying on a line. She bought him a small wheelchair to keep him mobile around the big house. She wheeled him to the grand windows to watch the birds close by. In warmer weather, she would take him on the large verandas. He sat at the table in a booster seat for his first Christmas meal. He made his way to the Christmas tree and reached out for the colourful ornamental birds that stood still in his small hands without making a sound.

Anntell announced in late summer that she would be leaving Rocky Point. She was going to go to New York, and then to Montréal to study French. She said all this knowing that she had to get away from Alfie Johns, that she had made a fool of herself for his attention, and that she missed Arthur more than she ever thought possible. He had been part of their crippled lives much more than she realized. Why had she not spoken up in his defence?

She could have handled her father. She held the ace card and she knew it. She, and only she, always knew that her father linked her in some way to his departed father. She hadn't bothered to ask him why. He would have slipped into an aria of self-indulgence on how to stone grief to death with hard work. What could she have learned from this disclosure?

What she really had to get away from was the fracture in the Briar household, and the guilt she carried due to her own selfishness. She had cast Arthur off like a lost stitch. She had stood by and watched him being bullied, hoping he would defend himself. Against what? A death that came too soon, too suddenly for the words that nobody in the house wanted to mouth.

She hated the old walls where the antiquated art-work hung like an expulsion notice to its tenants. The oak staircases lamented under her footsteps squealing voices from the past. Had they ever belonged here? Here, her mother had been lured by a man who got what he wanted, but never really wanted what he got. Her mother became aware of that too late; her grandmother damn well knew what would happen. Poor Joseph, her father's final flaw; the incomplete project he could not chisel or plane into the perfect form. He had a second choice. He could have seen the potential in Joseph, instead he would keep him surrounded by this house of wood, and let nature take its course.

But Arthur sensed the old man's philosophy from an early age; his sensitivities were his father's collateral and Arthur ended up paying the price. She remembers the day her father died. Arthur had come to her room looking for a cigarette. Why had she told him he was too weak to stand up to their father? This was the moment when things had gone terribly wrong. The last thing she gave him was enough anger to take him to his grave.

Anntell kissed her brother Joseph on the head before descending the steps and into the waiting taxi.

"See you, little brother," she mouthed to Joseph, who had reached out and held onto the handle of one of her suitcases.

She kissed her mother and grandmother then turned without looking back. Rosie Briar watched the back of her beautiful daughter's head disappear as the taxi went down the lane, knowing full well that she had just lost another child. She had tried unsuccessfully to get Anntell to enter university. She had hoped Anntell's attraction to Alfie Johns would keep her closer to home for another year. She'd pleaded with her to give her future considerable attention, but to no avail. Anntell was always strong willed and determined, even as a child. She spoke her mind to anyone who would listen.

"Anntell, I always wanted to go to university. I spent years dreaming of it—the freedom would have been overwhelming. You can attend any university you choose. Why let that go?"

"Mother, there will always be universities for me to attend at some time or another."

"I didn't have the choices that you are presented with, Anntell."

"I can handle anything. Universities are over-rated."

"What about Alfie? Why not wait and travel with him? You have been friends for years, Anntell. He wants what's best for you."

"What's best for me is not what's best for him. What he wants to be, he already is. I'm surprised he hasn't asked you to pose for him with Joseph. One day, he'll hold a portfolio of our lives in his hands and hang us up on a wall."

"Perhaps he has asked, Anntell, perhaps he has. At any rate, he has a clear eye on his future."

Anntell shrugged her shoulders. "My future is not here; not in Rocky Point, not in this house. I hope you get out of the house as soon as you can. You can buy any place you want, Mother, or have a new one built. You deserve better than this. This house should be condemned or burnt to the ground."

Rosie Briar held her daughter in her arms. She had not held her this closely since she was a baby. She could feel the change in her slim body, its emptiness as light as a bird against the heavy events a body carries towards its own truths.

"I miss Arthur. I know we never appeared to be close, but it was there, Mother. I kept waiting for him to make his move."

Rosie Briar sank to the floor, her body as limp as a ragdoll in Anntell's arms.

"I am so happy to hear this, child." Her sobs were deafening, like the cries of an animal caught by its prey. Above, the fan hummed over the sound of her sobbing. "Life should have been much easier for my dear Arthur."

Anntell pulled her mother to her feet and sat her in a chair.

"He knew we would support him. But Arthur was sensitive; I don't know if he felt safe after everything that happened."

"What could have happened? Why didn't he feel safe? With your father gone, he wasn't subjected to criticism here. He took the car when all he had to do was ask me to let him get his license. There's more to it than I care to think about at the moment."

"Arthur and the old man were arguing the evening he died, Mother."

"That was just a way of life around here."

"It turned into a way for death, Mother. The argument was intense; Father developed chest pains and fell to the ground. Arthur didn't go for help. He was racked with the guilt of it."

"Why didn't he tell me what happened? I would have understood and protected him. Your father would have died with or without help."

What did she expect her mother to do when she revealed to her what Arthur had done. There were too many secrets in this house. She didn't want her mother hearing anything from strangers. She couldn't cheat her out of this one. She sat close enough to her mother to catch her reaction. "Arthur drove himself mad not over father's death alone. He brought school boys to Joseph's window to watch him beat on his drum. It cost them a quarter and Arthur his life. He said he did it to get back at the old man and Joseph couldn't get hurt because he wasn't aware of anything wrong. It's you he worried about. He didn't want to hurt you. He feared the rumours in the village getting back to you."

Anntell remembers the sound of a falling spoon, the scraping of her mother's brace against the chair, her overturned cup dripping tea to the floor. Brown rain pooling along the floor. The grandfather clock recording time. A murder of crows in the tall trees. And then her mother's voice. Slow, quiet, splitting. "He could have told me. I would have understood what anger can drive a person to do. It's like carrying a loaded gun and waiting for your best aim. My poor boy. My poor, poor beloved boy. I hurt you more than you ever hurt me."

17

ALFIE JOHNS WAITED patiently at the post office for his film; he'd sent it to Montréal for developing. He opened the brown envelope carefully and leaned back against the post-office wall. He felt like a child at Christmas. He was never quite sure what to expect. What his aim had been on a particular subject he had photographed. There were several approaches he'd take. Sometimes he'd concentrate on the limbs of his subject, the scarred knuckles and spider veins of the old fisherman on the Salmon River, casting his line like an invisible rainbow over the quiet waters. Or the muscles in the neck of a young pitcher on a built-up mound, the deadly focus in the eyes, the steely silent aim of intent.

He studied one photo for a long time. What held his attention was Joseph's mouth nestled into the fabric of his mother's blouse as though he were breastfeeding. Joseph lay sprawled on his mother's lap, his tiny legs spread outward like a child playing a game of frog.

His feet were bare. Rosie's head was bent, slightly, to meet her son's gaze. His finger twined in a strand of her hair that had fallen downward from her forehead. A ray of light behind them produced a celestial effect: mother and child in a precious balance of life and limb.

Another photo was of Isla Jones asleep in her rocking chair beside the hearth. Her hands were folded over her knitting needles. A small mitten, fully formed, lay on her lap. Isla's head rested on the comfort of a soft shawl on her right shoulder. A long braid, loosely bound, resembled swatches of wool draped for display down over her shawl. A ball of white wool lay at her feet like a bowl of dough waiting to be shaped.

He had captured Anntell lost in her world of words; her long lashes soft blinds over her eyes. She had not looked up from the book. The pages opened by a pair of long hands, part of the extended concentration of the reader. She was fully posed, but not for the camera. She soaked up the words without a blink. He had taken this picture a few days before graduation.

Anntell was in the library with her head bent low over the book. She knew she would have the place to herself; solitary mental self-absorption, a gift she gave herself. She was not aware that Alfie had joined her until she heard the click of the camera. She gave him a superficial dirty look, stuck her head back into the book and turned the page. They exchanged a few words before he left. He would keep this picture of her in his wallet for years.

Arthur Briar looked at the camera as one would the barrel of a gun. His eyes were frightened, distracted; a look of sullen despair clouding his dark good looks. His lips were parted in protest, a silent F held back between his perfectly shaped teeth. Dark curls smeared his forehead. His high cheekbones carved an elegant swerve in his face, looking for a way out of his torment through his own flesh. This picture was taken a few weeks before his death in 1969. Alfie would never show this photo to Rosie Briar, but she had its image implanted in her mind's eye forever.

Alfie kept these pictures in a cool place. They were to him darkness on the verge of light, a draft that needed a seal, barren limbs on a majestic tree, a song whose words were never memorized, and love when it strikes, burning into its own heart.

18

THE DAY ANNTELL left Rocky Point it rained. Alfie Johns felt as though his feet had stepped into another country. The people he met looked foreign to him, their names and faces not coming to mind fast enough for him to greet them personally. He chose not to speak, kept his distance and avoided curious information seekers.

In the store, a cash register sang out for payment, a young male worker ripped open a carton of detergent with a jackknife to restock a shelf, two small children tore open a box of cereal to get a free hockey card. Alfie watched the flakes fly in the air and land like sawdust on the floor. Their frustrated mother pulled them by the sleeves and rushed them out of the store. They left the card on the shelf. She was teaching her children not to steal. Alfie walked over to the shelf, avoiding the crunch he would make as he walked through the cereal. The hockey player was face up on the shelf. He turned the card over and read the statistics on the back. High scorer. Least penalties. Two Stanley Cup rings. Alfie added another statistic of his own: abandoned on a cereal shelf.

He left the store with his pop and walked to the woods along a path well worn by generations of mill workers. A few wooden benches were placed along the route. Sometimes the men sat on the benches to eat their lunches at dinnertime or to have a smoke on their break. Through the trees, the sound of the swelling brook came in cracked, dreary groans. This was Alfie's day off, but he needed something to do.

He had met up with Anntell at the train station. She would catch a plane in Halifax. Her back was to him when he saw her standing in the waiting area, her ticket in hand. Alfie checked the big black and white clock on the wall. He had fifteen minutes to try and turn their lives around. Anntell looked up at the clock and gave him her final answer. It was in her eyes, a dry well of despair. Alfie heard the hissing of steel on the tracks.

A man's voice called out from a loud speaker: "All aboard." A porter took his position beside the open door, after placing a small step on the platform for the passengers to embark. He held an umbrella above his head. The rain dripped. A silver pool at his feet.

Alfie walked Anntell over to the train door. Against regulations. There was some rule that required non-passengers to stop at some cut-off point. Perhaps it was at the platform door, he can't remember now. Loved ones belonged to the big steel beast once they stepped inside and were swallowed up in small compartments.

Anntell turned and tried to smile. "Watch out for them, Alfie!"

He could taste liquor on her breath when he kissed her.

He can't recall what he called back to her through the rising steam. How pathetic he must have sounded and looked, standing there like a wet dog. She may not have even heard his voice, his pleas. He hoped she hadn't. He noticed a white hand waving, a patch of red from her raincoat, a strip of her navy scarf. Anntell Briar came to him in coloured pieces like an unfinished puzzle.

Alfie walked up the Briars' lane later that evening. The rain had stopped. He paused as he neared the big house. He was not limited for time on this visit. No need to creep up to the geranium window to see Joseph. Two dim lights shone beside the porch door entrance. This is the door Anntell would have departed from. Alfie wondered if Rosie Briar had turned the lights on should her daughter return home after dark. Perhaps she believed Anntell would have a change of heart. She couldn't have her stumbling in the dark to open the door.

It was possible she was already there watching him move up the lane at a snail's pace. He didn't suppress the thought. She could be hiding behind the pantry door for safekeeping, and jump out larger than life. Anntell loved games of hide and seek; she was capable of anything. He might soon feel her arms around him in a tight embrace, and a flood of words announcing her new game plan. A smile returned to his face.

Alfie approached the door quietly. He would keep up the surprise and not let her know what he was expecting. He checked the coat rack in the porch to see if she had left her first clue: the red raincoat and shiny new red boots she had dipped into the waves the night before when they went for a walk. He had captured several shots of this christening. Anntell, with one boot under a wave and then the other. Twin dippings. She had stretched out her arms as the seagulls flew overhead. She believed it was necessary to carry a scent the way other people carry memories. Salt was good for one's physical senses. She swore she would never wear the boots again, never erase the stains of Rocky Point from her feet.

Rosie Briar greeted Alfie as though she had been expecting him. She had kept a plate of food for him and began to set the table with blue-and-white-patterned dishes. Isla greeted him warmly. Joseph turned in his grandmother's arms and reached out to Alfie to hold him. He nestled against Alfie's chest.

"I believe he wants you to put him to bed," said Rosie.

The kitchen had the air of a quaint country church. And they waited for something to start, for someone to step up and explain it away. But there was no Anntell behind the door or upstairs reading a book on this closing down of the day in the Briar household. Alfie turned his head slowly towards the pantry and glanced at the slit of the door where it met the hinges. All he wanted was a slice of the girl who left, a patch of colour leaking out, a soft sigh exhaling from her lungs like a swimmer coming up for air.

"Anntell called from the airport before she boarded her plane. She asked if you were here." Alfie turned towards Isla Jones when she spoke.

Joseph had fallen asleep in his arms. Alfie heard the soft murmur of his breathing rising in the silence of the big kitchen. A candle burned low on a shelf. An old grandfather clock cried out the hour. Rosie Briar sat near the kitchen window with her eyes on the long lane, coloured in shadows. She did not mention her daughter's name. Crying in silence was something she had done for years, like knitting or crocheting in the dark. Darkness was easier on pain. Her flesh bore the brunt of sexual anxieties, like a child on her way to the principal's office for a strap. She had never learned to keep her moans silent. She felt as blind as her mother, a silver fox with the weight of the trap over its body, its opening probed with a bullet of flesh.

Alfie suspected that Rosie knew that her daughter

drank. She had that worried look on her face as though a mother's intuition sounded an alarm bell in her ear. Anntell was as far beyond her reach as Arthur had been.

Alfie watched Isla Jones crisscross her hands in slow motion to wring out the pain in her joints. She did this without saying a word. Nobody mentioned pain in this kitchen; the word itself was forbidden.

Joseph stirred as Rosie led Alfie down the hall, the sleeping boy cradled in his arms. The aroma of cooked ham floated down the hall.

Alfie ate slowly when he returned to the table. He spoke quietly about the weather, his job, about anything that wasn't of any urgency. He could see pattern on the china dinner plate more clearly as he ate away at the meal. He was not really hungry, couldn't even remember if he'd eaten all day. Beneath his fork, a small blue boy ran in the middle of the plate followed by a blue dog. They were running towards a blue fence. A blue horse and hay-filled wagon stood beyond the fence. A blue man pitched up the freshly cut hay with a blue pitchfork. Alfie wondered where in England this quiet scene of country life portrayed.

"Is there anything I can do before I leave?" he asked Rosie.

"No, but thank you kindly," she smiled. "You must come again!"

Outside the house, Alfie could see the small light

that glowed above Joseph's bed in his mother's room. It hung there reassuringly, this star that wouldn't go out until dawn. He walked home at a deliberately slow pace. He listened for night noises. The shouts of anxious parents calling to children playing in the dark. Barking dogs. Engines revving, heading for Lovers' Lane Look-offs. He heard the call of a hoot owl as he walked along a heavy patch of evergreens. He stopped to listen to its low, haunting pitch calling out like a mother in distress.

Alfie was not a superstitious person. He had shrugged at the old wives' tales Bertha Johns rhymed off in the kitchen. "Raw owl's eggs," she'd said, "are fed to children in Peru to protect them from drunkenness throughout their lives." She was making omelets at the time, with chicken eggs. Thinking back, someone must have told her that Anntell Briar liked to dabble under the cork. It was her way of letting him know she was aware of the Briar habits. That she had been on target with her prediction of the outcome of Arthur Briar's life. Who was next in the line to twist in her deep moral snare?

Alfie kicked at a mound of stones under his feet. He was angry at Anntell for leaving and not waiting until he could leave with her. He was not going anywhere on a Briar ticket. She had argued with him over this. "I have enough money for both of us for a long time. We can both go to school," she'd said. But he wanted no part of the money she had inherited. She did not comprehend that, handled well, her inheritance could be a beneficial income for her for years to come.

He was also concerned about her drinking and had mentioned it to her when she was sober.

"What are you rambling on about, Alfie? I have a refresher to cool off now and again. No big deal."

"It will be a bigger deal if you start to cool off too many times a day. This is what I'm rambling on about." It was all he could do for her at this point, but he was sure she would continue to drink without some form of intervention.

The night was broken by another owl hoot. The damn owl must have read his thoughts. It continued to hoot. He picked up a good-sized rock and threw it in the bird's direction. It stopped for a few minutes, made not a sound. He knew that the owl is a raptor, and it is illegal to hurt or kill them. The owl started up again; its hooting louder, more haunting than before.

Alfie Johns continued to walk home, tormented by a bloody hoot owl. He used fact as an antidote to superstition. Logic was in his favour. Hoot owls hoot at night. The owl was doing what was expected of it by nature. Then why did his heart cry out when he heard it? Why did it cross his mind that the owl could predict death? Even Julius Caesar's assassination had, reportedly, been forewarned by a hoot owl. Poor Caesar, perhaps he threw a stone or two at the owl while his assassins sharpened their knives.

Alfie smirked at the idea of a hooting owl as omen—it was pure nonsense. Bertha Johns would believe anything. Why did he even pay attention to her and her crazy omens? She would say anything to prove her point.

Bertha would be thrilled to hear that Anntell Briar had left town. She would ponder the future of the crippled boy, now, and the blind grandmother and poor Rosie Briar, with her braced foot and almost half of her family in the ground. But she would know better than to question Alfie about the state of the Briar household. Or to wonder aloud whose funeral would be next. He would walk out rather than answer her questions. They maintained a careful relationship. He was under their roof, as she and her husband knew, on borrowed time.

He lay awake for hours sifting through his future. The radio mumbled softly in the background. An announcer on the CBC, in a deep, serious voice proclaimed, "Two cells of the Front de libération du Québec (FLQ) have kidnapped British Trade Commissioner James Cross and Québec Labour Minister Pierre Laporte." The War Measures Act temporarily suspended the civil liberties of Canadians. This would have little effect on Anntell Briar, Alfie reflected. She was used to domestic liberties suspended on the homefront. Her mother, she had always claimed, had been kidnapped into marriage.

In less than a year, he'd have enough money to get out of Rocky Point. They could meet up in some far away city and travel the world. Things may have settled down for her after a year, maybe she'll have sought help by then. She might see things in a different light, or from a different bottle.

Alfie punched several dents in his pillow with his fist. One for New York, a couple for Anntell's jazzy friends she had mentioned to her mother as well in her phone call, and a few for his own inability to keep the girl here, where she would be safe with him. He knew what was going to happen before time would catch up with either one of them, knew very well why she was running and why he could not catch up to her. They were a family of runners, the Briars, except for Joseph, who could only manage a few feet at a time but still smiled through the pain. Had Duncan Briar ever taken a really good look at the boy, he would have known which of his three children could go the distance in the Briar compound.

19

ALFIE BEGAN WORKING at the mill in the payroll department shortly before Anntell left for New York. He walked the long hall to his office and stopped to check out the portraits of the Briar family studded to the walls.

Charlie Briar, Anntell's grandfather, caught his eye. He had a jovial-looking face, with a hint of the rover in his deep smile. He was a carelessly handsome man, with a look that no doubt left a trail of benevolent pleasure wherever he travelled. This look flashed from under thick brows causing sudden light in a dark room. A warm-hand-under-a-cold-blanket individual, who liked to act out wherever he may be in this world. Alfie imagined, had Charlie Briar been standing in front of him physically, he'd see a man well over six feet with broad shoulders and the handshake of a drunken giant.

So, it was a smile that sealed the gap between father and daughter, Alfie realized, as he stared at the portrait.

It was his father's smile on Anntell's lips that Duncan Briar held on to for the lost security of childhood. Something he himself had created to keep his father near. What was poured into the well of good hope for a happy life had taken a mere six years of his young life. Rowena Briar forced her son to ignore it until it faded from view forever when he was ten years of age; and then, unexpectedly, it re-emerged on the lips of his beautiful daughter.

Beside Charlie Briar is the portrait of his wife, Rowena Briar. She is wearing a wide-brimmed hat with feathers floating in a spiral at the back. Her dress is satin brocade with a matching coat, wrapped around her round shoulders like a matador's cape. Her eyes are intense, as though she had cautioned the photographer to follow her instructions and not to mar her appearance with shoddy lighting and poor quality film. Or else. A strikingly handsome woman, with a face she clearly kept out of the sun—her high cheekbones windswept and pale, faintly hidden beneath the rim of her hat; her wide mouth devoured her smile and would have no occasion to return it in a hurry.

Poor Arthur had inherited his Grandmother Briar's striking looks, through no fault of his own. The Stewart genetics poured the mould in Rowena Briar's favour. Had he looked like his grandfather, Charlie Briar, life may have bestowed on him the sentimental and economic value of the mill, and a father who would have reinvented a fort where the world around him was always safe in its warm blue haven.

The portrait of Duncan Briar is of a young boy of twelve or thirteen years of age. He had his father's broad chin and his mother's wide mouth stretched above it in a deep scar scowl. His hair was parted in the middle and forced down each side of his scalp with some kind of sleek oil to drown his natural curl. No twelve- or thirteen-year-old businessman needed a head full of curls. He was groomed to look the part, in a pinstriped suit and wide tie held down by a tie pin. His pale hands gripped the arms of the plush seat. A child trying to get out of a barber's chair on the day of his first haircut. His smile was vacant.

In his eyes lay the rest of the story. They held a rusted, worn-down look, staring straight ahead. Waiting for the click of the shutter, the sounds of a Christmas past, the roar of a lion, a father's footsteps, the clanking of ice in a glass of lemonade, the slow walk to his father's bedroom to keep him warm, and the funeral that robbed him of his tears.

There are no portraits of Duncan Briar as an adult, no trace of the man who had no desire to be bolted down again to the prize his father had willed to him, the Briar Mill.

Alfie Johns stood back from the portrait. He wondered why Duncan Briar had not removed this portrait of himself from the wall. Perhaps this is how he saw himself, pinned, bolted and waiting, always waiting for his fort. He had left the mill in his early thirties, paid someone else to keep it going and turned his hand to shipbuilding. People sought his workmanship from across the country and abroad. He received them cordially, set his price and left his signature deep in the wood of the great bows. No craft or boat built by Duncan Briar had ever hit rock bottom. In business matters, success never failed his hands.

At home, these same hands rummaged through a parcel of cold, vulnerable flesh that produced three offspring bearing his name. He had left his signature trademark with a woman who had never seen him fully exposed. Duncan Briar made sure his wife never did see him undressed. He stayed under a sheet to perform. Only she was exposed.

These same hands had never held his youngest child. Un-mouldable, Joseph was too awkward for a craftsmen's grip. Duncan looked at the bundle in his wife's arms, and saw proof of weakness in his own manhood. The child would be kept apart from him and from the staff; his downstairs room was never entered. It was referred to as the storage room. Duncan Briar made his instructions perfectly clear.

This is how Duncan's life is remembered by those left behind. What is left for them to add? Nothing but the occasional shift of earth on his grave, left still without a stone bearing his name. And she, Rosie Briar, is in no hurry to have one erected. Something must be said as farewell to the dead; she is well aware of the custom. But she cannot place it on a marker. It has crossed her mind to have this engraved on a stone, but she was never a woman who would hang her misery out for all to see.

She may have seen the first sign of deliverance from boy to man, had Duncan exposed himself to her just once. There is nothing left of the man than has not been identified in public. Public men have the hardest time with intimacy. Rosie Briar can attest to this fact. Upon further reflection, she realized she had never had sex with her husband, had only surrendered to him. She cautioned herself about such provocative thoughts as to what a real man offered a woman in lovemaking. This, too, was lost to her. Once she remembered that she had heard Duncan call out her name. It was like a half-whisper of sorts, in the wee hours of daybreak. She was expecting at the time. She thought he was ill when she heard him call out. She watched him unravel from his sheet like an Egyptian mummy as he placed his hand over her eyes. He did not say another word until it was over, and he casually reminded her that he was ready for his tea. She knew that, before the tea brewed, he would be up and in the kitchen: washed and dressed and ready for work, with only his face and bare hands visible. Why he kept everything else hidden was a mystery to her. Once in a moment of anger she had almost blurted out: "There is no need to keep it under wraps, Duncan, we have already been introduced."

20

ANNTELL BRIAR HAD been gone a month before Alfie received a letter from her postmarked New York. It was addressed to him at the mill. He looked at the envelope with anticipation. Was she going to tell him that she was returning to Rocky Point to wait until they were ready to leave together? His hopes were naked as he held it in his hand. He closed his eyes before the tear, the slice of the opener. He paused for another moment after the initial cut. Imagined her hands all over its smooth surface.

Her first sentence was as dark as what followed. In a drunken scrawl, she wrote that she was having a marvellous New York time.

My Dear Alfie,

Sleep is obsolete here in the big city when one is having such a good time. My friends are shocked that I hadn't left the misery of Rocky Point long before I arrived here in New York. Happy to hear you are keeping in touch with my family. Mother mentioned that my grandmother's house was up for sale. She was considering buying it for the sentiment of it all. I told her she should move back to her old homestead and get rid of the prison she now dwells in, for God knows what reason.

How long will it be before you get out of that hell hole and join the real world, Alfie?

Sorry I have to run. I'm meeting friends for cocktails at this wild bar that has pictures of Benny Goodman and Louis Armstrong clipped to their horns all over the walls. If you listen hard enough you can hear the music breathing through the cracks and come squealing down the walls. You'd love the photos.

I know that New York is a place you could wrap your arms around like a woman in need.

Until,
Anntell

Alfie Johns destroyed the letter. He could imagine the photos without ever seeing them. The sweet, hot horns, almost with lungs of their own, their genius rippling over the crowds. Their art was pure seduction; their music ripped wide and deep beneath the skin and gave the crowd their fix for the night.

He had no intentions of responding to Anntell. She was as self-centred as ever. Between the lines it was plain she was drinking up a storm. He had cautioned her about her liquid pleasures and failed. What could he do for someone miles away? He was not interested in the friends she had mentioned. He ripped up the letter as he walked along the path through the woods, and sent pieces of small white paper swimming in the brook.

He opened his wallet and looked at the photo of her he had taken in the school library.

Could she still find peace in the pages of a novel? What she read here in Rocky Point, she could read in New York. But he feared that, instead, she might settle herself into the roaring twenties and the blues, and not look back.

Unpredictable, reflected Alfie, as he struggled with his thoughts in the depth of dawn. He could go to New York and do what? Pull her out from between Benny Goodman and Louis Armstrong and wipe the jazz from her mind. She was getting into deeper trouble, and he knew it. She was still grieving, and he knew that, too.

He thought of her beautiful smile, the bridge between her and her grandfather that Duncan Briar crossed to keep his father's memory alive. Who was she smiling for in the big city, while the cocktails slid past her beautiful lips? Nobody around her would see the trace of Charlie Briar. They would not know about the boy Joseph, whose smile clung to his face like a blister.

Perhaps this is why people go deep into big cities, to bury themselves for a while. Big city mirrors throw back at you a distorted reflection. They tempt you out of your misery. The wide city sidewalks make room for you. The bars open their doors without a knock. Music breathes from cold, dead horns. And the real world, outside the door, is left for other people to sort out.

Alfie got out of bed and went outside. He stood under a crooked moon. He hadn't noticed it from his bedroom window as he tossed and turned. Anntell's scrawled handwriting crawled in the shadows on the ceiling. He recited her letter in his head, making his way down along the road near his home. Where was he going? He wasn't quite sure. He followed his feet to the main road and found himself standing in front of the old homestead of Isla and Rosie Jones. Beside the front door, a dim light bulb hung like a ball of white smoke. A few moths gathered around its glow. Dusty wings in motion. The house was run down. Discarded cans and rusty car parts now grew in the once-lavish gardens Isla Jones had nourished with her swift, clever hands. The man who bought it had rented it out over the years. An old country song crippled its way out from a small open window at the back of the house. George Jones's pure and haunting voice singing about loving some woman all over again today. Alfie tried to listen to the words of the song through the radio's static.

A "For Sale" sign hung in a front window. A broken

hinge on the front gate made it appear crooked, as though the house itself was on a slant. Yet it stood defiantly, its door hung on like the arm of a drowning man to a piece of wood. This house was fighting back after years of neglect, and refused to fall. Alfie wasn't sure who owned the property now. He stood for a while, taking in the frame that still bore the strength of Isla Jones.

He remembers seeing pictures of the Jones home in an old album. Isla and Rosie were seated on the front porch. Each held a bowl of freshly picked strawberries. Isla's eyes held a steely look, the colour of strength. She had the elegant face that comes to a woman of confidence.

Rosie was petite and lovely in a summer frock, still in her early teens; her body pointing towards puberty. She was aware of how the camera would picture her. A little shy, a little fuller, a little excited. She had let her hair down over her shoulders to advance her coming-of-age look. The brace on her foot was tucked under a chair.

"We were culling the berries to make preserves for the winter," said Rosie, as Anntell passed along her family's history with a sigh.

"Poor mother, all you ever did was work."

"It can be liberating; you should try it!" Isla's remark shot like an arrow towards Anntell.

Her grandmother's response amused Anntell, as she

rolled her eyes. Hard-working women have their own ethics scrawled on their faces, but she did not say another word about her mother and the liberating effects of the domestic aggravations she considered work.

There was a picture of Anntell and Arthur building snowmen taken near the Briar home. Arthur looked as cold as the snow. His face was iced in anger. The head of a snowman lay at his feet; it had fallen from its position because it had been placed too awkwardly on the body. Arthur appeared to be facing someone who was chastising him for breaking something valuable. Anntell, grinning from ear to ear, was next to her creation, which stood as erect as a stone statue. Her snowman was perfectly rounded; its coal buttons in perfect symmetry. On its head was a black Stetson hat.

There were several pictures of Rosie in her Sunday attire. In one picture she was wearing a blue crepe dress and white pearls. Her good foot barely touched the ground as she emerged from the car. She looked annoyed at the intrusion as she waved her white gloves to ward off the shot. In another, she wore a full apron over a blue dress. Standing in the pantry, awkwardly posing, Rosie was cutting into a deep blueberry pie. A bowl of whipped cream lay close.

Alfie had turned the pages of the Briar album carefully looking for a photo of Joseph. He turned page after page looking for one glimpse of him in the Briar circle. But the child was absent.

A cool breeze wrinkled the dark leaves in the trees. The old green hands trembled, clinging to branches. Alfie tucked his own hands in his pockets and stood for a while listening to the song. The radio gave off one more note before a voice cried out.

"Turn that fuckin racket off; ya never loved nobody in your bloody life!"

"Piss off!" A man's weary voice cried back.

"Shut up! George Jones never sang that song for idiots the like of you." The woman's drunken voice seemed to float up from the inside of a barrel. Alfie heard the sound of a bottle slamming up against a wall. George Jones kept singing, unaware of the turbulence his words added to the misery of the couple between the walls of Isla Jones's once-happy home.

21

ROSIE BRIAR SAT at the kitchen table, almost delirious with grief and longing. Her limbs and muscles cried out for relief. And to achieve this she would have to close down her brain, close down the visible pain in the living flesh she faced daily. Her son Joseph and her mother. How could she leave them alone? It was hard to tell if the living or the dead offered up more pain.

She had positioned four bottles of aspirins around a jug of water. "Ring around a Rosie"—this was her new game of late. There were no prizes at the end of this game. Through the jug of still water, she read the magnified instructions on the two bottles facing her. *Relief from arthritis and rheumatic pain. Keep out of the reach of children.* Something angered Rosie; she thought she'd read *not recommended for grief.*

When she looked out the window, she believed she saw the faces of her two lost children staring in at her as if she were playing a game of Hide and Seek with them. She took some comfort from the fact that

Alfie Johns held the emotional map to her daughter's heart, and she longed to question him. But there was nobody she could ask about Arthur. Anntell had never mentioned Irene to her. Perhaps, had she told her, her mother would have searched for the girl to thank her for loving Arthur. There'd have been comfort in the fact that someone had reached out to him in a way never possible in the Briar house.

When would Alfie be leaving Rocky Point? His departure would cause Rosie great stress, would leave another void for her to fill. Alfie was a big brother to her precious Joseph. The boy's limbs seemed to unlock when he was present. Joseph reached out for things, for arms to cradle him, for spoons to feed him, and for Alfie Johns' mouth to thrill him like a live bird perched close enough for him to touch the music between his teeth.

She had a long mountain to climb. At the immaculate hour of midnight, when she should have been sleeping under a half-moon and a sky freckled with stars, Rosie Briar swung her lame foot out from under the table and swore. She did this in silence, considering her lameness an appendage to her suffering, like everything else in her life. Her foot had fallen asleep and she removed the brace to massage her limb. Looking down, her foot reminded Rosie of a child's soft, white glove that lay on the floor. It was an inch or two shorter than the other, yet it was not an ugly limb. It did not frighten her. She had not considered her foot anything but what it was. It left its own impression on this world, according to her mother.

She can't remember having bouts with pneumonia as a baby. She wasn't told until years later why her mother sent her cousin, who had lived with them for a time, to stay with their grandmother, when Rosie was diagnosed with polio. He was carted off in the night and came occasionally to wave to her at the kitchen window until she was stronger.

She remembers when she was five and she wanted desperately to climb into the tree house with her cousin. With his encouragements from the branches above, she had made it as far as the third rung on the ladder before her mother's hands gently pulled her back down. At school, she sat back on the foot of the big hill and watched the other girls skip and swirl their way to victory with stones and ropes. It looked simple enough. On weekends she practiced in her backyard when her mother went shopping. Slowly she had progressed to a lopsided skip and the first three squares of the hopscotch before her foot began to nag her.

She played a game she'd made up for her own pleasure. She would sit with her back against the wall and move her feet in and out along the floor in front of her, stopping suddenly to look down at which foot was out front to be declared the winner. Little foot won its share, and was awarded a prize of painted toenails. She had never even told her mother about it. End of her secret game, Big Foot and Little Foot, if her mother found out; she needed to preserve her strength, she was told.

Rosie Jones knew her limits earlier than most. She would never complete a game of hopscotch, or a game of double-dutch. But she could study hard and land a soft job, something that didn't require two strong feet. Her quick brain would do the walking for her. And she had already become quite a seamstress in her own right.

"'Strength.' Pretty word, isn't it!" Her angry outburst floated around the kitchen at this hour. She doesn't have the strength for games anymore. And there is not a drop of nail polish in the house for the winner. Anntell took all the colours with her when she left.

And what, if anything, did Arthur leave behind? She is not sure. Anntell had Alfie help her remove everything from his room. It is a mother's prerogative to go into her dead son's room and look for memories. But she has not turned the knob on his door, touches it only, gently, as she walks by, in the same manner she touches the tips of Joseph's fingers. Leaves her colourless fingerprints, night and day.

Rosie shoved her brace under the table. Took another look out the midnight window and drew a deep breath. What she had always prided herself on was long gone. She had lost her strength the day she married

Duncan Briar. She had relinquished it, with the cup of tea she brewed him after he'd consummated their marriage.

She could not blame her mother's silver eyes for this part of her life. It was she who had been blind to what Isla had pointed out to her. Isla had pleaded with her to stay away from the man. How she had wished her mother's arms could have pulled her away on her wedding day.

But now Rosie has the ability to do the one thing she has wanted to do for so long: move out of this dreary Briar house. She will buy back the old home, have it renovated and add a sunroom and large veranda for Joseph to watch the birds from the back garden. She loved the old house. It was full of possibilities, surrounded by buttercups and an array of wildflowers. Someone might even wave to people through the kitchen window again.

22

ABOVE HIS HEAD, Alfie Johns watched a shooting star split the night sky, like a crack in a plaster ceiling. When he was in school, he had always had an interest in what went on above his head.

Wish upon a shooting star. He knew it was something Bertha would believe in. She lived in a wish world. Perhaps, when the offer of a child was made to her, she'd wished for a girl, an illegitimate girl. Someone she could wreck her feminine and hostile skills on. Keep the hem of her daughter's wedding gown unmarked until her wedding night. He does not want to think of the misery a young girl would have had to cope with under Bertha Johns' star.

The caseworker was dead, but there had to be records somewhere. Between the pages of the Old Testament, he had learned that his biological mother was a fighter. She never wanted to part with him. This determination could bode well for many women. It had worked for Rosie Briar. She had never given up on Joseph; despite her husband's wishes, she would never part with her son.

In the last few months, Alfie began to piece together a portrait of a woman he had never met. She would be in her later thirties now. Did she have blonde curls, set loose and dangerous in summer fields? Shorter now, perhaps. Tied back if she were cooking for a family. Her face could be oval shaped like his, with a few lines etching around deep-set eyes, resembling those created by a small twig in fresh snow. Was she concerned to see her youth at its fading point? Did she spend her spare time searching the faces of young men with curls dancing on their brows and a lost look in their eyes?

Alfie stood back and looked at his first sketch of what he thought his mother might look like now. She smiled back at him with full pink lips. He added a slight blush to her cheeks, and deepened the blue in her eyes, giving them an intense persuasive glint that a woman on the hunt would possess. Had she forgotten about him in her busy life? He somehow knew this was not the case. He never thought much about his father, or wondered if he was even aware that she bore him a son. Alfie concentrated on his mother. He sketched her with light brown hair and green eyes. Drew in a slight dent in her small nose that gave her a distinctive appearance. He left her without a smile.

He sketched her with long straight blond hair

tucked back behind her shoulders. This was a side profile of the unknown Clare. He graced her with a strong chin with a deep dimple. High cheekbones elevated the face of the woman with dignity and self-assurance. Another sketch of her was as a woman with a long braid coiled around her neck like a scarf. She stared straight ahead, her blue eyes contemplating the face of someone approaching. Her bottom lip drooped in awe. He imagined the question on her lips when they would cross paths: "Are you my son?"

He tucked his sketches under his mattress and bid his beloved Clare a goodnight. What would he say to her on their first meeting? "Clare, it is so lovely to see you." No, that somehow sounded too casual for a woman who walked into his life from between the pages of Bertha Johns' Bible. He would have to lighten the meeting, add an ice-breaker. It would have been easier if he had found the letter between the pages of one of Bertha's cookbooks.

Perhaps he would offer her a meal, take her to a fine restaurant to catch up on their missing years. He could tell her how they met years ago between the pages of a Bible. This would bring a smile to their faces. He would say how much he had admired her perfect penmanship, and tell her of the comfort he took from her desire to fight to keep him as her own. He would offer all the intimate parts of his life to her. She will be anxious to know these things, he believes, and in her mind's eye she will try and figure out how all of these things could have eased themselves into the beautiful mind of her seven-pound boy.

He would offer her a deep smile and tuck her close to his beating heart and wait to hear her voice call out his name.

23

ROSIE BRIAR HAD the wounds of her old home licked clean and bare before the buttercups bloomed again in the summer of 1972. A sale was in progress for the old Briar home to a young couple from Virginia. They loved the stark silence that filled the big house, they exclaimed. And the lake that sprawled within walking distance fueled their desires to spend as much time as they could in Rocky Point.

A 20 x 20-foot sunroom was being added on at the back of the Jones house for Joseph. Alfie Johns stood beside the road and watched as a work crew piled the debris from inside the home. Busted lamp shades were thrown to the back of the dumpster. One leg from an old cast-iron headboard stood out from the top of the heap like the rusty barrel of a gun. Alfie steadied his camera on the striped-down studs of the house as the crew drove away with the loaded dumpster.

Behind him a sinking orange sun cast a glow along the beams. A couple of stone masons were sizing the back wall up for a fireplace. It was a Friday and the men wiped their brows as they looked over at the heap of grey boulders resembling a small craggy mountainside that rose from the ground. Alfie caught the silhouette of the men at the foot of the rising stones in his lens. This would make a great homecoming gift for Rosie, thought Alfie. A new beginning at the foot of her own mountain.

Rosie Jones spared no expense on the old home. She didn't have to anymore. Duncan Briar had made a fortune and it wouldn't take a fortune to get the old place in shape. She wanted to have it returned to what it was before she left it. She knew the house had good bones. Her father had built it himself; his Isla, along with Rosie's grandmother, had measured window sizes for the curtains and planted the seeds that would soon bloom again under Rosie's green thumb.

"It's like going home," said Rosie to Alfie, as he rocked the nineteen-year-old Joseph in his arms by the big fireplace.

Isla smiled in her rocking chair by the fire. It wasn't a smile of joy or excitement. It washed over her pale lips. A piece of music she knew once a long time ago, and remembered sweeter words lived beyond these walls.

Joseph watched his mother's lips move and reached out a small hand to catch her gentle voice. He took great pleasure in listening for her words and locking them in his closed fist. He shoved his fist into his mouth and made a swallowing sound.

Alfie tapped Joseph on the head as a reward for making his mother smile, and placed him in his wheelchair, while Rosie went into the pantry to get Joseph his molasses cookie. Joseph ate in small bites, pieces placed on the tray of his chair. Rosie had had someone in to teach her how to do daily exercises with Joseph. He was taken to specialists and watched carefully for small changes in his condition. Beneath his warm sweater, his frail bones crackled beneath the deepening wheeze in his chest. He was confined to his wheelchair for fear of a fall. Alfie noticed the dark circles under Rosie's eyes, deep and severe rings that forecast an approaching storm. She understood her son's condition.

It was good she was moving back to her old home. She could leave her ghosts behind for the artists to capture. There was no reason to stay here. She had felt for months, now, that she was living in an unclosed grave. Above her head, she listened for the sound of feet and rain and traffic. Below her head, memories spoke. It was possible. They started off slowly, the dead. They whispered to ease their voices back to full range. They came calling when she least expected it. They asked for directions. They had left things unfinished, unloved, without respect, without warning; they complained to her late at night.

Duncan Briar's voice came at Rosie as bruising before the actual punch. His words battered her skin. He wanted what he had always needed the most, love. He knelt at the foot of her bed like a child afraid of night noises. He pleaded with her for a second chance. He dropped the names of his children like pennies in a wishing well. She watched the water expand in small circles, drowning each penny as his big hands reached in to save them.

Rowena Briar's wrinkled beauty resembled an iconic relic. She slid up to Rosie's pillow and pulled on her quilt. She demanded what she had always wanted: something hemmed up in a hurry. "I have been jilted," she cried in a raspy voice. "A woman will always lower a man past her knees when she is jilted. I want my black, silk dress shortened when he goes down into his grave, the miserable bastard."

Arthur's voice came in the loudest from outside her bedroom window. Unreachable, Arthur didn't bother to come inside. He was always begging for help on the edge of the cliff. His voice sounded much older than she had ever heard it, the stammers gone. She listened to his pleas and her heart pounded in fear. These were paralyzing moments; her limbs went dormant. She tried in vain to reach out and catch him—but to no avail.

It was her mother who heard the ghosts in Rosie's voice. She listened carefully for the whispers from her daughter as she went about the house. Rosie mumbled under her breath. Sometimes she was very angry. At times she heard her stumble into the furniture and weep. She heard her call out to Anntell as she puttered around the pantry. Isla Jones had trained her senses well. She could smell trouble. Even taste it. She was going to get help for her daughter. Something she should have done years before, she scolded herself. And Alfie Johns would be happy to help her. She would have to speak to him when Rosie was in town.

There was no use saying anything to that daughter of hers. Whenever Anntell called, she was drinking. She would be heading for Paris in a week or so, she claimed. The girl was going to end up like her grand-father Briar. She would die with a bottle in one hand and a man holding the other.

Isla Jones kept her thoughts to herself. Poor Rosie was saddled with enough troubles. She didn't need another convoy of agony on her mind. Alfie Johns was their saving grace. He was wiser than his twenty-one years. The way he took to Joseph. And his love for the girl never wavered. Isla wanted to ask the young man about his plans for the future, when he would be leaving, but she remained silent. Alfie watched Isla's face. He could read its frowns and downward contours. He knew what she was thinking about Rosie and about Anntell.

Joseph broke the silence by pounding lightly on his

tray. He listened for the sounds his small fists made to come back to him as he looked around the big kitchen. The two women in his life were silent, listening for sounds that would never return.

24

ALFIE BEGAN A new sketch of the woman he had never met. Her hair was long and thickly twisted in a dangling coil. It fell between her shoulder blades outlining shadows. Her eyes were partially closed with a slice of blue coming through like river water under melting ice. Her mouth scowled. Perhaps she had said something she'd wished to swallow back.

Alfie stared at the sketch for a long time. The woman he was looking at was Anntell Briar. Now there were two missing women in his head, running through his mind along different paths and different moods. How could he have imagined that his mother looked like Anntell?

There was no way of contacting Anntell in Paris. Her mother expected a postcard as soon as she arrived, she'd promised. Anntell made it clear that she would not phone until she was back in North America. She had Montréal circled on her map. Her tongue would be French within a year, she'd boldly stated. "Au revoir, Mama."

Alfie didn't expect to hear from her at all; he hadn't bothered to answer her New York letters. It still angered him that she had left her mother in such a vulnerable state. Rosie Briar's accent was grief. Her words trimmed with defeat.

He couldn't wait for Rosie to move back to her old home, away from the haunting memories of Briar Lane. Isla whispered her secret concern to him when Rosie went to the back room to check on Joseph, after Alfie tucked him down for the night.

"She doesn't close her eyes on the darkness, Alfie. I hear her roaming around all through the night."

Alfie watched Isla's face as she spoke. Her mind was sharp and clear.

"My Rosie would not leave me, and I could never leave her." Tears sprang from her white eyes. "But I must get her help, Alfie. I don't have to explain the situation to you. I am grieving for my grandchildren in my own way, but for her..."

The kitchen was hot as confusion. Alfie knew that it was purposely kept warm for Joseph and Isla, an insulation for thinning bones. He looked at the stoic woman wrapped in her thick shawl. Her pale face steeped with the dignity of an aging cleric summoned to even life's imbalances.

"I'll be happy to see her settled back into her childhood home, Isla. There is someone I can speak to about grief counselling for her. "

"You are a wonderful friend, Alfie. I know, at your age, you have the world to explore. Don't wait around here for Anntell to return. Her world is spinning out of control." Isla Jones's face appeared strained by some memory she could not reach, perhaps the thought of the young Anntell in her arms listening to a long-ago story, or the chords of a lullaby dancing in her head.

"She's still drinking." Alfie's voice carried a warning across the room. Perhaps he should have said nothing at all.

"Grief has many caterers, Alfie. Drinking was one Anntell had even before Arthur died." Isla Jones ran her hands over her sightless eyes to erase the image that crossed her mind. "She was always a different child, clever and quick, as you well know. Spoiled rotten by her father. And Rosie was a divided mother," her voice weakened, "caught between caring for a precocious child and a troubled son, and another constantly threatened with being carted off to an asylum."

"I had known the situation for a few years, Isla. Arthur was more transparent than he imagined." Alfie will not mention the geranium window. The seeds of that part of their lives need not be sown into this present grief.

"You should have met his other grandmother, Rowena Stewart. She could have curdled the blood of a lion with just one stare. The woman was incorrigible. She believed she had it all, the pompous fool: a rich, handsome husband and a brilliant child; there was enough meat for her ego to chew on, until she cut to the bone and was defeated. She believed pride was a congregation for the wealthy only. But she withered up and died like the rest of us will, and was buried from an empty church when she did."

Alfie's mind wandered to the photo of Rowena Stewart on the Briar Mill wall, and thought of the contrast with Isla Jones. She'd fallen asleep against the back of the rocking chair. Her socks overlapped at the toes as her feet draped the footstool like an over-stuffed woolen toy. She looks tired in her wooden perch. Her night sleep, no doubt, interrupted by Rosie's wanderings.

She is too old in her dreams to change what can't be changed. And her daughter is too broken to recognise dreams from reality. What difference would Anntell Briar make in this house at the moment? None. Asking her to help would be as useful as asking a drunken sailor to save you from a sinking ship. Joseph is the transfusion Rosie and Isla both require, his slight thump keeps their hearts whipping away at their grief; they cannot see that the job is Joseph's and his alone.

Had it been possible to photograph this scenario in front of him from the beginning, Alfie Johns would go back to Charlie Briar's wedding. He would look for the glee, or the glare, in Rowena Stewart's eyes. The camera doesn't lie. It steals the images that lies betray. He thinks that he would have liked Charlie Briar. Charlie and his anxious look, a big man with a big heart, looking to love someone deeply.

This is what it comes down to, when a man loves his child more than his wife. It is developed here in cold, hard misery. No man wants the burden of a woman who competes with their child for love and affection, a jealous, handsome woman bolted to the Briar wall by her own selfish will. How they met cannot be blamed on the laws of attraction. A daring man was cornered in the eye of a more daring woman. The new teacher in the village, well bred, well travelled and well aware of the man watching from the corner of his eye; she was the one who invited him in for the full view.

part

TWO

25

ALFIE JOHNS SAT behind his desk at the Briar mill and watched a stack of grey smoke shoot arrow-straight up in the air and mingle with a dark cloud in a bank of low clouds. He unlocked his desk drawer and took out a file. Work was up to date on his latest project. He was calculating a lumber quote for the new school to be built on the outskirts of Rocky Point; he began to shuffle some figures on a blank sheet that he could adjust for an additional lock hold on the tender. He shrugged his shoulders at the idea of the young minds filling up the classrooms of the school. Would there ever be others like Anntell or Arthur Briar walking the halls? He blotted out the idea and went back to the page.

Alfie Johns was growing restless. Nearing twenty-three years of age, his feet ached for new soil. He longed for the sight of warm ocean waves and cold-blooded sharks smiling into his lens. Ancient cities offering up their treasures through the dust of time at daybreak, old war fields that cried out in pain when you walked over the bones of their dead. He read about a village in Europe where the villagers would never walk after dark through these weeping open fields.

He had moved some months ago into a small house close to the mill. He enjoyed his freedom. Now and then he kept company with young women, who upon occasion, began to plan nests in his small abode and in his heart. He watched their eyes skirt the floor plans, imagine the walls in rainbow colours and covered with pictures. They glanced at the photography books piled up on the floor.

"Alfie," they'd sigh, "your walls look anemic. Your whole house needs colour."

He could almost hear the sound of sewing machines stitching up puffy curtains for his empty windows. He never took any serious interest in the women, some of whom he had attended school with for years. They voiced cautious hints about the Briars, about why they believed Anntell would never leave another footprint in Rocky Point again. He bid them a cool goodnight when he walked them home later. They were never invited back to his sparse nest.

Alfie sat in his house and looked out through an empty window. All those women were right about one thing. He himself began to believe that Anntell, bold, beautiful and bewildered, would never again be seen in Rocky Point. Had she been here, she would have thrown a towel over a window for privacy. Anntell Briar could care less for empty walls or bare floors. Her presence would fill up any space. Her mouth could add the colour.

The dour conversations under Bertha and Wilfred Johns' roof, he erased from his mind. Bertha and Wilfred refused to speak to him when they met. They crossed the street when they saw him approach. This amused him; he welcomed their spiteful silence.

Rosie Briar and her mother were settled back into their family home. Strapped in his wheelchair, Joseph was wheeled out to the back deck to get a look at the colourful shapes that nature provided for play. His limbs were supported by vests that anchored him upright. His small hands reached out to catch the wind.

Isla Jones took daily walks around her new old home, holding on to rails that guided her back to her past. She paused at the door of her sewing room, now Rosie's bedroom, and listened for what could have been the sound of her sewing machine with its needle inching along the seams of an elegant gown for her beautiful daughter. She sat beside Joseph on the deck and filled his head with leftover lullabies. Joseph could no longer hear them, but she sang to him in her strongest voice. Isla held his hand to her throat as she sang. She knew vibrations were required to let Joseph feel her voice. She understood it, the secret voice in the pulse of Joseph's veins. His hands danced.

Rosie watched all of this from the open door of the large deck. On centre stage, in full view, were the two loves of her life. She watched their shrinking limbs entwined in song. Joseph rocked slowly back and forth as her mother sang an old ballad that her husband's grandfather had brought from Wales. For a few minutes, Rosie Briar stood still, and then sprang free from the labour that grief weighed down on her. A slow breeze combed through her hair. The sun came to her as a gift, lending her its light warmth. She moved her feet to her mother's voice. She had not danced for so long, now she simply followed the breeze and the song on her mother's tongue. She felt free.

Rosie had not heard from Anntell in months. It came as no surprise. Her daughter had always lingered in her own gaps and then sprung back like a boomerang to twirl at her feet. She made no apologies for her actions.

Anntell had promised a letter to follow her Paris trip when she arrived in Montréal. She was bilingual enough to read and order from a French menu after only a few weeks in France. She could inquire about different routes around the city, she informed her mother. She was going to enroll in French classes to get a conversation going with people who looked at her like stunned sheep when she asked a question about the weather. She never mentioned returning to Rocky Point for a visit, although she did inquire about the family and asked if Alfie was still working at the mill.

Rosie thought it best not to mention any of this to Alfie. He had not asked about Anntell since she'd left for Paris. Rosie assumed he had moved on in his life. He lived alone now, and went about his own business, keeping company with other women causally or otherwise. It was his life to live as he pleased. She was indebted to him for staying with her mother and Joseph when she attended grief-counselling classes, and visited her private therapist in the city.

Two of Alfie's photos hung on the waiting room walls of the doctor's office. Rosie was pleasantly surprised because Alfie had not mentioned them being there. On the far wall, a black-and-white photo of a pair of delicately shaped feet caught her eye. She felt drawn to them in a manner she could not explain. Perhaps it was their perfect balance, the strength they exuded. She imagined the miles they could cover without a dent altering their firm beauty, the quick reflexes held beneath their smooth skin. The girl's feet were perfectly straight where they lay, slightly parted to invite in the sun between her thighs. The second photo was a coloured winter scene. A path ran long and deep. On a snow-laden branch, a lone blue jay looked down at heavy footprints indented along the path, as if it bid their owner farewell on his journey. Something in the photo evoked a deep melancholy in her.

Rosie knew that Alfie stayed around Rocky Point to keep an eye on her family. He loved Joseph. He held long conversations with her mother, and was kind and helpful to her. He longed for Anntell's return. He had adopted them as his family, she was convinced, and they had certainly welcomed him into the fold with open arms. Alfie had asked her permission to photograph Joseph, Isla and herself. He presented her with the photo shortly after they moved back to the family home. She had him hang it above the fireplace.

His photography was growing more popular. He was invited to galleries around the country. He had just returned from an exhibition out west. The boy had a great talent; she was very excited for him. But it was a talent that would pull him away from Rocky Point, and she was not ready to let him go. Not with Joseph in such a delicate state.

She had not been ready to let Arthur go, either–he just went. You can't change character in midstream. She was angry with herself for Duncan's unwillingness to love his sons. What had she done to counter it? Kept them close to her apron strings whenever he was near. She secretly feared that she had Alfie Johns under her wing as a substitute for her sons, especially for Arthur, who could have given life a go with his father gone. He would have grown into himself, she thought, even got himself a girlfriend; he was handsome enough to get any woman's attention at his age. How strange she believed this, as though Arthur would just walk down the street with his goods looks and instantly be sought out by young women looking to be loved. He was broken, and she knew it. It would have required years to mend him. Damaged children turn into damaged adults; his father was proof of that.

Rosie Jones knew the first time Duncan Briar touched her that he would touch her again and again in the same painful places. He never once told her that he loved her. He was a man who spoke to himself, and he, alone, answered. The longer she remained, the more his touch wounded her. She was as soft as lamb's wool beneath him the day he married her; her sacrificial duties came with a contract. She would remain tender.

26

"**GRIEF IS COLOURLESS**, slow moving fog banks ambushing the mind's eye." This, Rosie Briar blurted out as she wrapped her arms around her shoulders for comfort; an initiation of sorts, in a stranger's office— she had just been introduced to the doctor

"Nice to meet you," Dr. Simon offered, with his hand extended warmly. They meant nothing to her, other people's greetings. She was here to please her mother; she owed her this much. She had overheard her conversation with Alfie.

For months after Arthur's death, she had a hard time remembering the exact colour of his eyes. "Where they blue or green?" She murmured softly to no one in particular. "Had his hair turned darker when he became a teenager? Or was that just his moods?"

Shortly after his death, she had Anntell put all the pictures of him away. She preferred to know the past in the present in other ways: to remember the smell of cool air in her kitchen that Arthur carried in from the lake, the scent of salty air in his wet curly hair when he came in from the sea; to touch the doorknob of his bedroom door, and imagine holding his hands. When she moved, she had the door handle from his room in the Briar house put on her new bedroom door.

"Do you think this has been cathartic for you, this constant reminder?" asked the doctor.

He was about her age, with a deep frown tagged to his brow in multiple lines, Rosie observed. Slightly built, he walked more slowly than a man his age without any physical disabilities. Rather, he seemed to pace himself like a preacher approaching a pulpit to deliver the whole nine yards of grief, thread by thread. His straight black hair pushed back without a part, a draconian character on stage waiting to exhale his first line. Yet his voice was calm and soothing when he spoke, choir trained no doubt, to keep his alto range alert and perceptive to the withering voices he listened to.

At times, he saw flashes of the once beautiful woman come through her anguished pain like a wild mare unbridled. She'd toss her hair back, startling in her defiance. Perhaps defiance and death trigger the same response. She had not said aloud, that, despite the circumstances, she was glad that her husband was dead. His grave was still unmarked, but beside it stood a marble monument to Arthur's memory. Carved deep into the stone was a lake surrounded by trees and a lone figure with the moon lending it its light.

One son dead, a daughter immune to reality, and another son harnessed to death's immortal chain, a chain that grew shorter by the day: Rosie's family was falling at her feet. She was well aware of what lay in her future. Death would take life's downfalls and infirmities, and lay them away forever. No more of what Duncan considered clumsy messes or laziness, things for a man to contend with in the run of a day. He could reshape Anntell, or so he'd believed, lure her away from the bottle with his own code of ethics. Duncan Briar stayed away from liquor; Rosie imagined his mother had laid down that rule. She wouldn't put anything past a woman who kept pictures of rifles on the parlour walls, including the one that Charlie Briar used on that fatal night.

Rosie searched for an answer. Before her eyes the shiny brass doorknob turned, opening and closing a door softly, then more loudly after an altercation with Duncan. She could hear heavy footsteps going out the kitchen door and Arthur's deep breathing whistling through his nostrils as he shuffled towards the barn. He was on an angry errand, rustled from his bedroom to get something or other done on command.

And then Duncan appeared in the kitchen door, his face flushed. His eyes misty with anger at the cousin of regret he referred to as Arthur. His knuckles white, clenched to resist the impulse to strike out at something. He dared not to strike a six-foot-two man-boy and expect to walk away unharmed.

"That boy and the other one would have been better off wiped from the womb before they were born, if I had any say in it," Duncan exploded.

Rosie came out of the pantry with a pan of molasses cookies cooling on a rack for Joseph. The cookies spilled to the floor when she lunged at her husband. "Leave my sons alone!"

She pulled back, perhaps surprised that she had defied him after so many years and that she was fighting back for her sons. Or she was no longer afraid of what he might do to them?

It was then that Isla had picked up the poker and struck it savagely against the stone hearth. Duncan mumbled under his breath, and left the house in a rage. Rosie watched from the window to make sure he had not gone into the barn after Arthur.

The doctor cupped his chin in his left hand as he observed the woman seated across from him.

Rosie referred to the children as hers, even Anntell who, without a doubt, was her father's favourite and the primary love of his dysfunctional life. Anntell had played on his weakness like a violin. Note for note. She excited the loneliness of the only child in him, and gave him a playing field into which he wandered in his arrogance. He avoided touching her physically; it may have weakened her to have a father who coddled her, a pet lamb branded with the Briar code.

She would have made a better sister to him than a daughter. She was cocky and loud, and Duncan Briar saw no need to restrain a mind as gifted as hers. He had no one to compare her to, except his father whose smile was bred upon her lips. Exchanging one smile for another, Duncan felt a special connection with his daughter. In dark moods, he contemplated her aggravation towards him. Duncan Briar lacked the youthfulness that youth required to father someone as strong as Anntell. Yet they played the same game, admittedly with different rules; he convinced himself of this for years.

Arthur, he believed, fell from the Stewart branch of the family tree, and picked himself up far enough to sink his teeth into his father's wealth; Duncan was sure Arthur expected to thrive on his mother's affection until his father's will was read.

Rosie Briar spun the hard wheel of misfortune with the hand of innocence well hidden under a soft Sunday glove. She had others to protect. Had she been as verbally groomed as her daughter, had she been as well read, had she listened to her mother's advice and stayed away from the Briar compound, the crushing wheel of Duncan Briar's empire may have ground to a halt.

27

THE THOUGHT TO change his last name to Clare came to Alfie Johns before his first photography exhibit on the west coast. He had submitted some of his photos to a national competition; the first prize was an exhibit at a rather exclusive art studio. It was easy for him to slip into the pocket of a new identity. The name "Alfie Clare" carried with it a beacon of light, a glimmer of someone whose talents he firmly believed had been slipped to him as a parting gift, wedged in between his closed little fists when nobody was looking.

He had several sketches of what he imagined his Clare would look like should they ever meet face to face, and that he hoped might have some resemblance to her at the year of his birth. The day he entered the agency that handled adoptions, he carried a briefcase full of these sketches. The lady he spoke with eyed the faces as if she were checking out bullet holes on the side of her house.

"This was over twenty some years ago?" she sighed under a smoky breath.

"Twenty-three, to be exact."

"That's an eternity in this business." The woman tried to break Alfie's gaze.

It was evident to him that she didn't want to deal with anyone's past. She was not a back-tracker. She appeared to be sixty years of age or more, and tired of trying to weld mothers with sons and sons with mothers. Gone were the days of pregnant girls at her door begging for just one touch of a hand or a foot, perhaps a photo, before their babies would be taken away. There were rules. The mother was forbidden to see the child after its birth, something about attachment becoming lethal. Fucking rules. Oh, the bondage of pink and blue.

The caseworker's hair was a weather-beaten grey, hanging frizzled with split ends down to her shoulders. Not a strand to indicate what colour it might once have been. She was rather thin, and wore a crimson streak of what could pass for leftover passion—or the memory of it—on her long, homely face. Her dull blue eyes, alarmed, scanned the images of the woman. Something remembered? Something she wished could be forgotten was eclipsed in her eyes. She turned away from Alfie, pretending to concentrate on the old black-and-white television in the corner where a news anchor delivered the deaths and casualties of the war in North Vietnam like a eulogy.

She turned slightly, and walked over to the television

to change the channel. From his trash can, Oscar the Grouch was screaming "Get out" at someone. *Sesame Street*, it seemed, cheered her.

Alfie reached out his hand and picked up the sketches he had shown to the woman. She glanced towards him without meeting his eye.

"What did you say your last name was?"

"I was reared by a couple named Bertha and Wilfred Johns. I have changed my last name to Clare. I found a letter from a caseworker that stated the Johnses would agree to rear me as long as there would be no interference from my biological mother. I never did find out if an adoption took place. My biological mother's first name was Clare."

The woman turned towards the window, staring into the emptiness. It was frequent company for her in her line of work. Alfie knew she was hiding something. Her body growled inwardly. She placed a closed fist over her stomach to try and settle it into silence. A scalded voice spoke to Alfie Clare.

"If they agreed to rear you, it sounds like a private adoption. That would have gone through a lawyer. What did your parents say about your mother?"

"Very little. I was wondering why a caseworker was mentioned in the letter. One would assume it had some connection with an agency, and since you have been around longer than I have…"

"The answers you are looking for aren't here." She

was looking to Alfie's left as she spoke, as though some-one else was in the room. "I don't recognize any of your sketches, young man. I am sorry."

"The letter came from here. That I am sure of, Miss...." She didn't offer her name. "Did this agency send children to foster parents who later requested adoptions?"

"I'm sure we did, but I have no recollection of your case, Mr. Johns or... Mr. Clare?"

"It's Mr. Clare, should you bother to look up my records and change the name."

The woman coughed loudly and hid her face behind a polka-dot handkerchief.

Alfie walked down the street and made his way into a darkly lit bar and grill. The waitress served him a beer in a tall chilled glass. She was about his mother's age, with a strong-boned face that seemed a prerequisite for the job in a loud, sweaty bar. She walked with a confident swagger calling out to her patrons by their first names.

"Hey, Joe, you ready for another draught of foam?"

There were posters all over the walls. Old local hockey and baseball teams smiled back at the photo-grapher. Their threadbare uniforms added to the atmosphere of the place. A jukebox in the corner slid out a conveyer belt of country and western hurting songs. The waitress returned with Alfie's meal and smiled between the music. She had a deep smile. Deep enough to reach the pain in his gut and let him relax for the first time in a long time.

"Bon appétit, my son."

My son. He had never heard the words spoken to him. He ate slowly and ordered two more beer. He felt at peace for a moment.

A small muddy window faced the street where he walked into the bar. A few buildings up he could see the agency he had visited. He watched as the door opened and the woman he'd spoken with emerged and lit a cigarette. She paced back and forth in front of the building. She appeared agitated as she butted out the cigarette with her shoe and went back inside the building, closing the door.

Rain slid down the window creating little mud slides on the sill. Alfie finished his beer, paid his bill and walked out into it. It was a warm rain that fell on his shoulders. He removed his jacket to cover his briefcase and its valuable contents. He smiled to himself, wondering if Clare liked the rain as much as he did. He could see a small light on in the agency office as he approached. The woman had her head hung over a black folder. She seemed to be reading furiously. Alfie tapped on the window with a firm fist and a shower of papers flew high in the air. The woman rose slowly from her chair, still agitated by the sudden pounding. Through the corner of her eye, she caught Alfie's face staring in at her.

He stood there in his wet shirt just looking in. He didn't say a word. He didn't have to. She had seen it all before. The urgent need to know who you are in this world and what name rightly belongs to you.

She was relieved that she had locked the office door, not because she was afraid of the young man with the gentle, blue eyes, but because she was afraid of telling him what she knew about his mother. Bertha and Wilfred Johns did take the baby as a foster child. A year later they applied for, and were granted, adoption. That miserable Bertha Johns had to test everything out like a recipe. The woman remembers not liking them, and wishing that the child had been adopted by a warmer couple. She had even mentioned it to the supervisor who approved the adoption. A couple of years later, the child's biological mother had died from some illness. The father, in this case, had never been identified.

When she looked up again, the young man was gone. No doubt he'd be back someday. He seemed far too intelligent to let go of something this pertinent in his life. She scolded herself for lying to him. What difference would it have made now? She was retiring soon. She'd always hated this job of hiding children from mothers and mothers from children. And why in the hell didn't Bertha and Wilfred Johns tell him the truth from the beginning.

A cautious emotion stirred in her chest. She could

go to him after her retirement and reveal the truth. Something about Alfie Clare appealed to her. He dared to be honest. To be formidable. He wanted the truth in its simplest form.

Alfie dropped his briefcase in the back seat of his car and laid his head against the front seat to rest. He was awakened a couple of hours later by a light tapping on the car window. Behind the tap, the sodden-looking caseworker stood in a wet grey streak of gloom. Her hair clung like paste to her head. Her mouth opened like a slice of yellow flesh. Rain pounded on the roof of his car. Alfie bolted upright, as if he'd been tossed from a cold dream, and lowered the driver's window.

"I've been watching you from my window. I didn't want to disturb you, but it will be getting dark soon. I want you to come back to the office. There is something I think you should know."

Alfie ran after her in his shirtsleeves. He didn't even remember he had a jacket with him.

The woman sat a cup of coffee down in front of him.

"Your visit took me off guard," she began. Her voice was more in control. Confessions have a way of charming the truth and unleashing the tongue. She cleared her throat and took a deep breath.

"I was not the caseworker when your adoption was granted to Bertha and Wilfred Johns." She stopped and lit up a cigarette. "I wasn't in favour of it, myself.

Didn't care for the couple. Mind you, they weren't criminals or physically abusive. It was their personalities..."

"My mother," Alfie cut in, "I want to know about Clare. I don't give a damn about Bertha or Wilfred Johns."

"You are a very intelligent young man, Mr. Clare, and you possess a great talent. I have seen your work in magazines. I knew who you were when you walked in here earlier."

"Where can I find Clare? Did she ever come to look me up?"

The woman got up and walked towards the window.

"You should have been informed years ago that you were legally adopted." She turned to face Alfie in a cloud of smoke. "Your mother was very young, fifteen or sixteen at the time. As I recall she was a very bright young girl and quite feisty. She left town shortly after giving birth to you and attended university for a year or two before her...."

The taste of pain, sharp and bitter, rose in Alfie Clare's throat. He swallowed and swallowed; it slowed to a crawl, but it would not go down. Only out. Before he reached the bathroom bowl, he was kneeling in his bar-and-grill meal, his three beers, and the realization that his Clare would only ever come to him in a sketch. He lay on the cool tile floor, his knees tucked close to his chin. He tried to figure out what part of his body was without pain, so he could lean on it, get up and get the hell out of this place.

Alfie heard the woman as she circled around him. The tips of her shoes stopped two or three inches from his face. "I made some fresh coffee. Please come back to the office with me."

Alfie leaned on one elbow and rose to his feet to reach the sink. He ran the cold water for a while before splashing his face into its cold fluid drip. The woman sat behind her desk as he walked back to the office. Outside, the rain had stopped; the sun lounged low beneath a blue haze.

He stood directly in front of her as his thoughts sank into each crease of her pleated face. She looked bone weary, but calm. He apologized for the mess in the washroom and asked for a mop to clean up.

"That won't be necessary. The cleaner will be in later."

She pointed to a steaming cup of coffee and directed Alfie to have a seat.

"I was going to wait until I retired to give you the information. But I don't care anymore. I'll take my chances. I've always hated this job."

"I want to know what happened to my mother."

"She passed away from a lung infection. She was eighteen. I know she was attending Dalhousie University studying law. She was hell bent on finding you."

Alfie watched the setting sun sink below the waste of the lake. A sad hum of wind ran along the window-pane. The woman's voice came through the air, a soft lament against a hard reality. He took a deep gulp of the coffee. For a moment, he wished he had not come here. He should have kept Clare on the missing list, where he had placed Anntell. There's always hope in the search.

He heard the sound of his own voice; its edgy, awkward tremble as he spoke like a five year old whose mother disappeared from his sight on his first day of school and never returned. Puff. You are on your own, boy. Anxiety separation. Death separation. The litter of life compressed in the bold black-and-white letters of the alphabet on his imaginary blackboard.

A is for anxiety.

B is for biology.

C is for Clare.

D is for death.

"Where is my mother buried?"

"In Halifax, where she was from; she was sent here to have her baby. She was an only child. She, herself, was adopted. The graveyard is directly across from St. Mary's Basilica."

"Her last name? I'm assuming they didn't take that from her, too," Alfie cut in.

"Her adopted name was Clare Lauchlan Moore. I don't have any information on her mother's name. Her adopted parents have passed away. I believe that is the end of the line on this case."

The woman's face had the look of a witness who took her oath seriously and delivered the goods for the sake of a social conscience. And he assumed that she knew he would have been back again; he had, he suspected, inherited Clare's determination. The worker was close to retirement, but closer to exhaustion. He felt a certain pity for her. She looked in need of someone to take the time to appreciate her. She could add this to her internal resume, the fact that she had freed him from the bondage of his questions.

Alfie left the office, taking deep breaths of cool air before he reached his car. He saw the small light go off in the office, and watched as the woman walked along the street in a shuffling, seesawed motion, an emotional drifter on life's highway. For a moment he wondered if he should offer her a ride home. Then thought better of it, and drove, slowly, away.

28

ALFIE BOXED HIS head into the middle of his pillow. Its wings stood firm and white as though he were lying on a goose. At the foot of his bed, he had turned the light on above the black-and-white photo he had titled "The Geranium Window." It hung high above his bed in its grey frame. He had it blown up to a 20 x 30 size for full effect. His first and last image from that day. He had included it along with "Summer Feet" and another titled "Under Moonlight," a photo of the Briar Mill rising from a prison of darkness in billows of smoke.

It rained on the day he had taken the picture of Joseph's window. He'd stood back under an umbrella to protect the lens from the rain. Joseph was directly behind the geraniums, the outline of his face partially visible between the petals of the third and fourth geraniums—one eye exposed, perfectly clear, curious and poised directly on the lens. Alfie waved to him. He watched as one small hand unfurled like a flower. He would have to get a few shots quickly. The boy tired easily, but on this day he stood as firm as the stems.

"Good boy, Joseph, good boy," Alfie whispered under his breath as the raindrops beat against the glass.

Alfie walked over to the window and smiled at the boy. He stood still as Alfie reached into the open window and groomed his face with his hand. His smile fell into his opened palm.

He was struck by the outline of the Briar Mill with its thin lines of smoke rising towards the moon. Nothing escaped his eye.

Alfie realized that the competition would be tough. He waited for months to hear back from it. He would be thrilled, he told himself, with an honourable mention, an honourable impression for the people he loved exposed in fragments, Joseph's eye and Anntell's feet, to world-class judges. They would have noticed the photos' sensitivity, their sculptured angles. An amateur would be at a loss to submit to this league; he would at least be judged on merit.

Alfie rose from the bed and walked over to the picture of "The Geranium Window." So many years had passed, so many changes had occurred since this photo was taken that day the Briars were away at church. Back then, he had not yet entered Duncan Briar's home. Joseph was still in his room with his drum; he had made his way to the window when he heard the music Alfie played for him. Anntell was lost in her fiction and poor Arthur was just simply caught in the middle of it all. And he heard it time and again. But the most potent talk between father and son was yet to come; the one that would eventually scare them both to their deaths.

Alfie studied the photo carefully as he ran his hand over the visible eye. How much did Joseph really see on that day he went to visit with him? The slanted rain, the man with music dripping from his mouth on that second visit. Did it sound like rain to him, or a visiting bird? What did a sound hold for Joseph Briar? Did his father's voice frighten him? He never appeared frightened by anyone or anything.

Perhaps it is what one listens for that makes all the difference. Music on a Sunday morning, day and night bird calls interrupting the wind, rain washing the backs of leaves, a makeshift drum from his brother's hands filled with sounds from under his own, or a mother's voice hiding inside his ear. Joseph Briar was blessed with all of these sounds.

A large brown envelope arrived by registered mail on a Friday. Alfie stood in the middle of his rented house. He waited for a minute or two before he opened the envelope. Its official "yes" or "no" still sealed between his fingers. It had been almost three months since he had mailed the photographs to the competition. The blue jays in the white birch trees and the crows on the telephone wire watched, to claim a share of the victory, for they, too, had been captured in Alfie's lens.

He opened the letter slowly and carefully began to read it.

Dear Mr. Clare,

We, the jury of 1974 Fieldmen Competition, have the honor of congratulating you as our grand prize winner. Some of the comments are presented herein regarding all of your entries and the overall winner.

"Under Moonlight" evokes the savage interference of environmental elements captured in collision with nature's lunar feast....

"Summer Feet" has the raw magic of daring leisure blushing for the sun....

"The Geranium Window" reflects a provocative and brilliant eye on the eloquent reign of nature's obedience drenched in full bloom and has been chosen as the grand prize winner.

The letter fell to the floor from Alfie's hands. He watched the blue jays and the crows scurry to a spot in the grass near the ravine. A skirmish broke out for some prize or other. A flurry of white, blue and black feathers flew upward. The winner, a lone crow, pecked at the ground and hurried away, something dangling from its beak; the crow landed on a telephone poll and raised its head.

29

ALFIE WAS PLEASED with this opportunity, although he was never comfortable with the word "talent." He remembered an old fisherman he met when he was a child, who made intricate carvings. "You have a great talent," he told the fisherman, while admiring the treasures the man kept on a wooden shelf in his fish hut: a replica of a lighthouse intricate in detail, Alfie opened and closed the small door just to hear it squeak; small dories rowing fishermen, complete with their oilskins and boots, out to their fishing boats. Alfie's favourite was a line of seagulls perched on the edge of a wharf with bits of cod dangling from their beaks.

The old man smiled without looking up from his carving. "I have a great knife; it does most of the work. You have to keep your eye in focus, lad, and a steady hand. The rest will settle in. What is left over is what you attribute to talent."

Years later, he understood what the old man meant. He had beautiful subjects and a great camera: these made his work easier. But fame came with its own price. He would have to extend his boundaries—present public showings; give interviews that he'd rather not have to give for articles he wouldn't want to read; travel. The thought of travelling bothered him the most, while Joseph was still part of his life.

He made his way to visit Joseph and his family. Alfie heard their voices on the back deck. An easy banter of soft conversation met him as he turned the corner of the house and walked up the back stairs.

Strapped into his wheelchair, Joseph watched Alfie approach. He coiled his small hand around Alfie's finger and pulled it close to his mouth. A chorus of shrieks played on his tongue. His eyes filled with laughter.

Rosie touched the boy's head. "You like it when your friend comes to visit, don't you, Joseph?" She smiled at Alfie. "That's his way of trying to greet you with a kiss. He's very clever, my boy."

"That he is, Rosie. My friend is clever, indeed."

Alfie chose not to mention the letter he had received, although the victory that it presented belonged not only to him, but also to this family. He would mention it to Isla first, she was the stronghold. His plans were still to be settled, and Rosie would be troubled by the prospect of his leaving; Joseph was becoming more delicate by the week.

Joseph kept a steady eye on his friend as Alfie sat

beside Isla with a cup of tea. A soft band across his forehead kept his head from jutting downward. He was losing more muscle control now. A small tremor appeared in his hands. A gripping knot tightened in Alfie's stomach as he looked into Joseph's eyes. He hadn't noticed the slight film that crept along the rim of his left eye towards the iris. What if he were going blind? He had already lost most of his hearing. What would Joseph do should he not be able to see his mother's face again, his loving grandmother and the birds that came near him in flocks?

Rosie noticed the concerned look on Alfie's face. "He had a cold last week and an infection in his eye. The doctor wasn't too concerned about it. Stick around, Alfie; I'm getting supper ready!"

Joseph's vision was clean on Alfie again. Clean and sharp, as if he was taking him in whole, staring directly into his eyes. The intensity of Joseph's look made Alfie uncomfortable; he turned and watched as a lone crow landed directly on the railing to his right.

Jesus, he was not a superstitious person, yet a cold sweat swam out from under his collar. He remembered the owl that had tormented him the night after Anntell left Rocky Point. He reached down for his camera and aimed it directly at the bird. He could capture it in flight. The lighting was perfect. Three or four white birch trees rippled in the background. A white ocean of limbs waved towards himself and the crow. The bird stood as poised as a peacock, its beady eyes watching Alfie's every move. Motionless, defiant. Alfie wanted to throw something at it, to make it go away. Instead, he diluted the depth of field on his camera and concentrated on the bird. They were eye to eye. The crow taking him in, too, intently. It fluttered its wings as if to take flight, but did not move. The damn thing was posing, or begging for something. Alfie continued to click in succession. He couldn't imagine why the noise didn't frighten it away. The crow dipped its beak into the wooden railing. Alfie continued clicking until it rose and scurried off into the white trees. A black flurry.

"He is very friendly when he gets used to you," Rosie told Alfie, when she saw him watching the bird. "I'm working on him to eat from Joseph's hand." "Scarf," as he was christened, had been hanging around for weeks and took to resting on an old silver scarf Rosie placed beside Joseph's chair. The crow ate from her open hand.

Joseph watched the movements of the bird with heightened agility in his limbs. Scarf accepted the boy's enthusiasm with a slight "caw-caw." He pecked at Joseph's feet for a few stray crumbs. Joseph followed the bird's performance. A few weeks later, on a spring Sunday afternoon, Joseph held up his hand with his mother's help. Rosie dropped a few seeds in his palm. Scarf landed gracefully on the arm of the wheelchair and dined from the offering. Alfie Clare knelt back a few feet away with his camera ready. He focused carefully on the opened hand, the seeds, the crow's steady eye on the feast; it was the last photograph he'd ever take of his precious friend, Joseph Briar.

30

HE STOOD BEHIND the window of a downtown Halifax hotel and watched the city come to life below his second-floor room. A couple of stevedores stopped for a minute to light up smokes, then kept walking towards the pier. A city bus crawled along the street and stopped with a searing groan from the brakes. The driver had momentarily forgotten to let the passengers off. Tired-looking women and men stepped out and scattered in different directions—office workers and salespeople and hospital workers. A knot of university students huddled together in a sheltered storefront. Alfie observed the tallest young man in the group. His hands jutted up and down, in and out, as if they had a language of their own and were demanding the group's full attention. The others stood passively by.

Alfie imagined Anntell amongst this group. She would have the upper hand. She would bruise the conversation to suit her opinion. "Who gives a fuck for

Kafka and his metamorphosis? He never even bothered to explain the insect."

He turned from the window. A flash of red caught the corner of his eye. He stood for moment, looking over at the plant. Its red petals made even darker by the dimly lit room. He had noticed the geraniums in the window of the florist shop as he walked along Spring Garden Road shortly after he arrived in the city the night before. He had purchased the strongest-looking plant on the shelf. He hadn't made up his mind, yet, whether to plant it on Clare's grave or leave the plant in the pot. He hadn't even thought about what kind of flowers he would place on her grave, but a warm feeling came over him when he saw the geraniums. As if Joseph's eyes were on him, watching his every move.

Alfie lay back on the bed to decide how his day would begin. He wasn't hungry. Breakfast was not in his plans. The graveyard was only a short distance from his hotel. Perhaps he should just get dressed and go; he could shower when he returned from Clare's gravesite.

His limbs felt like lead when he moved to get up. He took a hot shower to limber up for the journey. Alfie's mind raced. What else could a man with a plant do on a day like this, but find the resting place of the woman who gave birth to him. He would dig a small hole in her grave and plant the geranium, he thought. He slung his camera bag over his shoulder, placed the geranium in a bag, left the hotel and walked north.

Clare Lauchlan Moore's grave was on a hill near an old willow tree, almost hidden in its shade. A few branches formed a fan over her tombstone. Its marble stone looked like the door one would find on an old country cottage deep in a forest. A fairytale setting.

Clare Lauchlan Moore

1938-1955

Only child of Drs. Yantesse and Picket Moore

Loving mother of Alfie Caelen

Here lies our beautiful sorrow

Beneath the epitaph, incased in a glass frame, was her picture. Her blonde curls met slightly tanned shoulders; her blue eyes, a feast of calculated risks, impulsive showdowns with Yantesse and Picket Moore, no doubt, when she fought to keep her son. Her pink mouth was full and locked in a slight smile. The young girl who troubled death at the age of eighteen but succeeded in having her last wish granted: the acknowledgement of her son.

Alfie knelt on the grass and used his pocketknife to dig a small hole to the left of the stone; he would plant the geranium. The mist fell more heavily as he worked. He stood back and looked at the red plant against the grey marble. A soft breeze whispered and two petals fell in a graceful dance. The mist sneaked down through the branches and spiraled over the grave, a web spun and polished for the occasion; Alfie got out his camera.

This is not the way they should have met, but it was all he would ever have. He had no desire to seek out his grandparents' graves. They might have passed on by now. They had never bothered to seek him out. He supposed they had their reasons. At fifteen, with puberty for a guide, the cards had been stacked against Clare, no matter who dealt her fate. He had no desire to go father-hunting.

Alfie left the graveyard when the sun streaked the tombstones in slabs of buttercup yellow. He had an urge to turn back and watch dying rays of light fall against his mother's stone, but decided against it. A weight descended upon him. His shoulders slouched. He had closed the book on his fairytale images of Clare. He had, with a quiet ache, found where she rested. There was nothing more for him here. He would have the photographs, an image of beautiful sorrow developed from his passion, and a woman he never knew who had left him a message etched in stone.

31

BUTTERCUP YELLOW EVERYWHERE along the highway back to Cape Breton. Alfie Clare had never adjusted to wearing shades. He kept his focus clear on trips, and his imagination open for the next obscure shot. An old tree jutting out of a lake, sculpted by time and nature to resemble a dinosaur's skeletal remains. Two cranes, dipping beak to beak, formed the shape of a heart in the open water.

He hadn't bothered scouting the city; he found what he was looking for in the mist. It was a success, in a manner of speaking, this finale, with its dates and departures, its heritage and its official grief. He would not return. It was not like some exotic place or great book that people revisit for something they may have missed the first time around. He'd missed what he'd found on this visit for a long time. He had the photographs and her picture to work from; he had come close to capturing her real looks, but now he could fill in the blanks.

He smiled when he thought how much her impish look reminded him of Anntell: the impulsive grin, the feisty look in her eyes. They would have liked each other. And now Anntell was off to Spain, according to her last note to her mother. The running of the bulls would be on her list, Alfie assumed. There had been no mention of her going to college, where she belonged. He knew her well enough to know why she didn't bother to write to him anymore. She avoided questions; her mother had run out of them. All her journeys would be arranged from a bottle. And her so-called friends would be invited along at her expense.

Alfie was surprised that Duncan Briar's will had dropped such an extravagant amount of money into her open hand; Duncan knew how impulsive she was. Or did he really care? Men like him believed they could control life from the grave. His financial genius had been seduced by the smile that Anntell now turned into tormented laughter. And the more she laughed, the quicker she would get rid of the wealth. She longed to waste, not only Duncan's money, but also the image of the man himself.

The rest of Duncan's fortune had been left to Rosie: the mill, his shipbuilding business, his house, all his personal belongings, everything except his car. How ironic that was the one thing he left to Arthur. But Rosie had had other plans. She revealed to Alfie that she had meant to arrange driving lessons for Arthur, and buy him his own new car.

There was a pit in Alfie's stomach as he approached Antigonish—one that the quick stop at a fast food joint could not begin to fill, a suffocating loneliness, desire. He hoped Clare had had a chance to hold him just once. He had known her at her most vulnerable: inside her womb, he had known her love; she would have traced him with the warmth of her hands, have tried christening him with an array of different names. His insides churned in an orbit of troubled stars at her loss.

Suddenly, he had an overwhelming urge to make love to Anntell, imagined a raw passionate exercise. He remembered the sand sliding down her spine under the wharf, caressing her thighs as it fell back into the soft pebbles of sand. He wanted to fall into her, now, never to leave as she crumbled beneath him.

He imagined his mother, with her last breath demanding to have his name etched in stone along with hers. She would cradle him forever in her dust. Through the car window, he watched a young mother walk by, holding a small blond haired child by the hand. The boy was about two or three years of age. He clapped his plump hands as the red balloon he held wiggled freely into the air and landed in a small puddle.

32

DEATH AND ITS consequences can hold hands for years. This is what Alfie Clare believed when his phone rang at two in the morning and Rosie Briar's hysterical voice called out his name. He arrived at her home within minutes.

Joseph lay peacefully; his limbs unlocked, a shy smile upon his lips—a gesture, from death, toward his dignity. He was free of pain. Rosie sat in her chair by his bed, rocking furiously as she rambled through what sounded to Alfie like an old Welsh song. She didn't look up when Alfie entered the room. Isla sat close to Joseph and held his hand.

"Alfie, open the window for me, so that his dreams can roam freely!" Isla's voice was calm. "This is what my father taught me. A custom from the old country. Death never changes its rules."

Rosie seemed oblivious to the soft breeze that ran over Joseph's quilt.

"I knew he was very low last night," said his grandmother. "He'd had a rattle in his chest all day. Rosie thought he had a cold coming on. She refused to face it, though she must have known what was coming."

Isla made her way over to the sway of the rocking chair and stroked Rosie's hair. Rosie sat quietly for a moment, staring at the wall. She seemed to be listening for something. She mumbled a few words, but the only one audible was "Anntell."

"I sat by him for the better part of the night. I knew, I knew," Isla said to Alfie, who kept watch for the ambulance from the open window. He had called for one, asking them not to put the siren on when they came to the house.

"I'll make Rosie a cup of strong tea." Alfie spoke softly to Isla, as though he may be disturbing something if he spoke up.

"Tea will do nothing. She's in shock. I can tell by her body's response to touch. She'll have to be taken to the hospital, the sooner the better. I'll be all right until you can come back."

Alfie followed behind the ambulance along the darkly covered roads that led to the hospital in Sydney. Shadows of trees and porch lights and fence posts and a lantern in an open field flew by. A blizzard of stars marked the night sky. Covered in a thick shawl, Rosie Briar sat quietly beside him as the lights from the ambulance flashed through the windshield window. Alfie knotted his grip around the steering wheel. It was the first venture Joseph had taken without his mother at his side. Inside the ambulance, his slight body lay strapped to a stretcher. Isla had insisted that he be covered in his quilt.

At the hospital, a kindly faced nun, dressed in white, led Rosie Briar into a quiet room. A doctor went in a few minutes later. Alfie paced the floor. From down the hall, he heard a wailing cry emerging from a newborn's lungs. In the back of his mind, he wished for this child, just entering this world, two happy, loving parents.

The kindly nun appeared in front of him like a spirit in a dream. She smiled warmly, but did not introduce herself. "Mrs. Briar has been sedated. The doctor has admitted her for bed rest. She is sleeping now."

Alfie thanked her and asked about the arrangements for Joseph.

"I assume you are a family member or a close friend."

"A very close family friend," Alfie nodded.

"His body will be taken to the undertakers in the morning; the family can make the arrangements with them. I rather doubt his mother will be able to attend his funeral. "

Alfie looked at the woman. She was younger than he had first imagined. Her green eyes wise and merciful, here to greet the precious bodies like Joseph's. She is the spiritual connection between life and death in this place. Alfie is not a religious person, but he is comforted by this woman's presence. He wondered if she knew the family. Everyone would have heard of the Briar name in connection with the mill. He decided not to question her. He would have to make most of the arrangements for Joseph's burial. There was little point in asking to see Rosie; the doctor was right about her needing complete bed rest. It was near dawn when he drove out of the hospital parking lot. He could see the black smoke and smell the sulphur rising from the Sydney Steel Plant as he turned for home.

The dawn began with a white smear breaking like cracked ice in the eastern sky and allowing the blue morning and rising sun to lighten the day. Isla was asleep in her chair when he entered quietly. Alfie decided not to wake her. He could tell that she had been crying by the swelling under her eyes and the mournful moans that fractured her breathing. He sipped on the coffee he'd picked up on his way home and slipped out on the back deck to catch a breath of air. He sat in the chair opposite Joseph's empty wheelchair. A Stewart plaid blanket was draped over the back of the chair, and to the left, near the front wheel, the silver scarf neatly folded and ready for the crows' next visit.

Where were the birds on this crisp July morn? No chickadees, no sparrows, no finches. Their absence baffled him. The sky and the trees were empty.

He was about to get up from his chair to check on Isla when the shadow appeared to his right. Alfie watched as the crow landed smoothly on the arm of the empty wheelchair. Scarf looked down at the seat where Joseph once sat. The bird cocked its beady eyes on Alfie before descending towards the silver scarf and began to peck at the threads for any speck of leftover seeds.

Alfie Clare watched the scene in front of him for a time, then his head slumped forward and he was weeping.

33

IN ROSIE'S ABSENCE, Alfie Johns escorted Isla Jones to the crowded funeral and laid Joseph to rest beside his brother Arthur. Their father's grave lay a few feet away, its green stretch of space marked by a small battered wooden vessel at the head of his grave. There was nothing to indicate the dates of his beginning or his end.

Hundreds of onlookers watched as Joseph Briar's small white coffin was claimed by the earth. They came from miles away to see the dysfunctional Briar family's plot of land, to mark the missing tombstone. They wanted to see if the young Briar girl had the decency to show her face after departing Rocky Point with her large inheritance. The crowd stood quietly as they watched the stoic Isla Jones, her head held high, being escorted through the green paths of the cemetery on the arm of the young man who had changed his last name to Clare. When people spoke to her, she called them by name. They looked directly into the eyes that didn't look back. They were astonished that she recognized their voices after all these years. Isla, sensing their surprise, knew more about them than she cared to reveal. The slight thickening in the waists of some of the brides whose gowns she had made many years ago, now standing in front of her with their offspring beside them.

Among the crowds were some of the young men Arthur had lured as school boys to his brother's window. Below a small hill stood Bertha and Wilfred Johns. They did not approach Isla Jones or Alfie. They had come out of curiosity, not sympathy.

After the funeral, at Isla's request, Alfie cleared out Joseph's belongings and packed them in the large shed outback.

"There's no way of knowing if Rosie will want them back in the house when she returns," she told Alfie. He agreed as he wrapped Joseph's belongings carefully and made special shelves to store everything away.

What he kept apart from his other belongings was the drum that Arthur had made for Joseph. He took several photos of it. This instrument had such a strong connection to Joseph's life, he gave it a special holding place beneath Rosie's bed. Perhaps, he thought, she could remember its beat.

A friend and neighbour, Charlotte, moved in with Isla to take care of things and keep her company, so Alfie was not there the day Anntell called and learned of Joseph's death and of her mother's hospitalization.

"She called out of the blue, from Spain," said Isla. "She said she had a premonition that something was wrong."

Alfie looked at Isla's lined face, with its deep composure. So many of life's struggles were written between those lines, and yet she withdrew from none of its sorrows. Her face bore a charismatic defense to tragedy.

"How did she sound?"

"She sounded like Anntell always sounds, in denial. She said she was expecting it at any time. She'd always known he'd never grow old with his infirmities. We all knew that life was limited for our dear Joseph. Still, I could feel her struggling. I know she feels responsible for Arthur's death somehow. The less she reveals, the more I know her." Isla drew a deep breath, "I asked her to call you."

"What did she say?"

"She said she'd see, but I doubt she can see much of anything, the poor girl."

"Do you think she was drinking?"

"I believe she thinks she's sober. But what you don't face today will face you tomorrow. I hope she is close to you when it happens, Alfie."

"I haven't heard from her for years, Isla."

This is all he can say. He cannot and will not tell Isla Jones what he knows, what Anntell is facing and will face for a long time. Alfie watched Isla's face. He knew her well enough to read her. He had noticed her particular skills at Joseph's funeral: her keen sense of whose voices met her ear; her ability to put time and place in order. She had filled the pockets of her mind with what sightedness would have provided her.

He watched her hands knead a white Kleenex into a pale rose, each petal growing out of her fingers, until the flower stood on its own between her thumb and index finger. The wind slipped in between the petals and opened them up, left the rose a song that only Isla could hear.

Alfie suspected that Isla knew what had happened on Briar Lane so long ago. She may have even alerted Arthur to the fact that deceit takes on a life of its own. Questions settle in your mind and clog your reasoning.

Alfie can imagine the conversation and how it might have sounded, back in 1967, after Duncan Briar's death. Imagines himself looking through the kitchen window of the Briar mansion: there is Arthur Briar dressed in something red. A long-sleeved sweater or shirt. He is alone in the kitchen with his grandmother. There is red, flaming heat in the hearth. Isla can count each crackle of the shooting sparks. Arthur's eyes are bloodshot from too many sleepless nights. Rosie has gone to the store with Anntell. Joseph is resting in his bed. Snowflakes gather on the window's ledge and slope into its corners. There is Arthur Briar pacing the floor. He can see his grandmother counting his steps. He tries to stop, but stopping is not good for him. He prefers to keep moving. It is harder to trap a moving object. He is agitated. The white dog could appear any minute. Isla can sense the boy is afraid and waiting; fear has its own waiting rhythm. She opens her mouth to speak, but Arthur is thundering down the hall. Checking windows. The damn dog can hear him whisper. She waits patiently. He is back and kneels at her feet and rests his head in her lap. Her hand roams through his hair.

"You can tell me anything, dear boy. I will carry your pain into the darkness." She speaks softly to Arthur.

Tenderness and pain confuse Arthur Briar. A soft and hard blow across the face.

"I don't want to hurt my mother. I shouldn't have used Joseph to teach my father a lesson. I'm glad he's gone, but if I'd helped him, and he'd died anyway, then I'd be...free."

"Freedom is not arranged, Arthur; it is earned." The conversation is hushed. "And should he have survived, you could still be free. People are separated by their behaviour and their desire to transform others into themselves. Not by love. Love is tricky, my boy. You always wanted validation from him, but it was your heart, the foreman of all emotions, that stayed to be mended."

Slamming doors and outside voices end their closeness; Arthur is on his feet. His red eyes search for an exit, and he is gone, off to his room with his grandmother's wisdom half asleep in his head.

Alfie was fortified by this woman every time he met with her. She spoke in even tones, an ocean of low tides. He had never once heard her raise her voice. She sat upright, her shoulders back against her chair. When she didn't speak, her body spoke for her. Her every movement contained a question and an answer. Her hands lent her vision.

Alfie noticed traces of Isla's strength in Rosie. They floated, like wisps of cloud, when she mentioned her children's names. She should have harnessed Anntell's stubbornness at an early age. Why did she leave Arthur alone to collect his own rage like a child in the wilderness gathering wild berries to fend off starvation? Who knows how much Joseph understood. If he understood love, then perhaps he understood the hatred his father had shown him.

And she herself, she had allowed what happened to happen; the so-called marriage equation, the so-called "happily ever after." The so-called "till death do you part." And death did its part before the end. Her end is still here. Rosie is still here. And she waits, still, because she still loves. Still believes she gave her love to three parts of the equation. Still hopes she has one last chance to hold her daughter again.

Life never ends where it begins. It ends where it is led.

34

ROSIE BRIAR RUMMAGED through spring's beginnings at dawn, eight months after her return from the Dartmouth hospital. She picked the heads off of dandelions and soaked them in a jar, ran a convoy of jars along her veranda. Yellow was one of Joseph's favourite colours, she insisted. She listened for the birds and named them accordingly. "Ruffles," the fat brown grouse, wandered up to the back step. The blue jays in the trees were referred to as the "Two-Tones" and the brown and white sparrows she flung seeds to were the "Toasted Marshmallows." Joseph's world.

And a few weeks later, sitting on the back veranda, she pointed to the empty space where Joseph's wheelchair used to be, and asked if he were still sleeping, even though she was fully aware that he had passed away. She circled her hand in the breeze and cupped it slowly, carefully. She wanted to feel something breathe besides her own breath. She placed her closed hand near her ear, opened it wide and smiled. It is not unusual, unreasonable, for grief to mime what memory has left behind. Emotional energy was the strongest force against the grief she still carried. It circled her. Colours caught her eye. For months, she lived in a world of colours.

She was confused by the birds' continued appearances. Why did they appear after Joseph had left the back veranda? She had no alternative but to feed them. It was her duty to carry on the ritual of seeds and sorrow.

The easiest thing for her at the time was to go backward. They were all there, the three of them in her backward world. She remembered them in brightly knit scarves and mitts, sweaters and caps. Anntell in a blue dress, in the back of the car on the way to church, it was silk, the Sunday dress she remembered, and how smoothly it floated around her body like warm water. Anntell hated it. Silk and satin didn't collect any space in her head, she'd complained on their way to worship.

Arthur loved red. He wore his red sweater until his arms grew out of its sleeves. He hated the dark suits his father made him wear on Sundays. The ugly striped ties that hung, noose-like, from his neck. Arthur didn't complain to his father. Rosie remembers the complaints reached her ears only when his father left the house.

"Remember, remember, Rosie!"

His voice streaked across the kitchen air and into the pantry. His tongue drowned in white spit; his agony black as rage. She reached for the chocolate cake to sweeten his pain. His arms folded her up and love returned. They sat facing each other at the kitchen table. Their cups full of tea going up and down, the small tinkling sounds of the cups hitting the saucers, an array of dark crumbs between them brought about laughter. Mother and son, laughing.

"Mamma, you hate him as much as I do. Why are we still here?" He had asked point blank.

"Because I love you. It is all I can do right now. How could I provide for all of you? Sometimes, Arthur, money is stronger than love. Your father could make life even more difficult for us. Until, Arthur, until!"

He could read the look in his mother's eyes. The possibilities of salvation should something happen to Duncan. But "until" was too late for Arthur Briar.

For a year after returning to Rocky Point from the hospital, Rosie Briar kept one hope alive: the return of her daughter. There was a silence between them that she could fill at any time. She reserved this for her night projects. Anntell came to her in and out of sleep. Her lanky, elegant frame tanned by many suns. Her tongue dedicated to foreign languages. She could teach her mother the newest syllables of travel.

Anntell would have to assert her new knowledge.

Change her accent. Alfie was still here. There were many possibilities for her travelled daughter.

"Do you think Alfie would stay here if Anntell returned, Mama?"

"I'm not sure, Rosie. He has a flourishing career. His work is very much in demand. He's off to New York in the next few weeks. He needs his own space to fill. Anntell has already covered hers. I'd love to sit that girl down and ask her why she believed she had to get up and go."

They were sitting out on the veranda full of summer sun. Isla Jones held her daughter's hand. She could feel the small tremors of new strength in Rosie's voice, her conversations growing longer about her children, her questions pertinent to the day's events. She was seeing her doctor every week. Their friend and neighbour, Charlotte, remained a permanent worker in their home.

Isla avoided the subject of Anntell's drinking. No need to parcel Rosie down with a problem she can do nothing about, especially when her own healing was so vital.

"I'm going to look after that young man, Mama; he has been so kind to us. I will put Anntell's money in trust. I know he will take care of my girl."

Rosie went somewhere in silence. She paused in the conversation and stopped talking.

Isla reached out and rubbed her daughter's hands.

They were cold as a child's just in from the snow. She did not speak to Rosie. Let her go to the space silence had beckoned her to. She needed this quiet time. Whoever was in there with her had to be left alone with her for the moment.

35

ALFIE CLARE CROSSED the border for his first American exhibition in 1974. The twenty-five-year-old, self-taught photographer was invited to Manhattan, courtesy of the International Center for Photography. The fresh-faced young man, with the serious eyes and innate talent, had caught the attention of a board member from the newly formed Center at his winning exhibition in western Canada.

The man spoke with a slight Irish accent; he introduced himself and then commented on the maturity and sensitive nature of Alfie's work. Alfie nodded politely and thanked him. A broad-shouldered man, nearing sixty perhaps, he walked with his hands behind his back. He stood in front of "The Geranium Window" for a long time. His eyes distant like grief, an old wound afraid of mending. He was old enough to be his father, thought Alfie.

"You live in an isolated part of Nova Scotia, an island, is it not? This place called 'Cape Breton'?" The man turned slowly to look at Alfie.

"An island indeed," Alfie replied, "although we've had a causeway linking the island to the mainland for years."

"Where would you have studied art on this island?"

"Behind the lens. I'm self-taught," Alfie grinned.

"Ah! No tuition fees! It's rare to see a self-taught artist produce this quality of work. Talent is a wonderful blessing."

"Thank you, sir, I consider this a compliment."

"The first of many, I suspect, young man."

"Are you a photographer?" Alfie inquired.

"Not at all." He laughed, "I've been steered away from anything that clicks for safety reasons. I'm into finances."

He asked for Alfie's card. Alfie scribbled his name and address on a piece of blank paper and handed it to him.

"You might want to consider having professional cards printed; they are a tad easier to keep track of, should one be requiring your address for future contact."

"I'll see to it, Mr. Avery."

As a result of his scrap of paper, Alfie Clare received a letter from New York. He was invited to bring up to eight prints for a joint exhibition. Several other artists would also be included. A christening of sorts for the newly formed gallery, the letter read.

Alfie hung several of his photos against the bare, white walls of his house. He wanted to be drawn once again into their "sting"—a word he used to describe the way his body quivered at an image he had evoked, held there until it came back to him in black-and-white stillness in his hands.

He decided not to take the picture of his mother's grave.

Joseph's small hand holds out an offering. His fingers twigged together holding a sprinkle of seeds. A river of tiny bloodlines crisscross his hand like a map. Directions, of a sort, for the pet crow "Scarf" to get to his feast. The vanished thrill from Joseph's lungs while Scarf feasted slid down the photograph and created an echo in the silent white room.

A flame in the hearth of the Briar house casts a glow on Isla Jones's face as she sleeps in her rocking chair. Her head resting to the side, her long braid of hair a ladder of strength down her chest, where she let her grandchildren climb with their fingers to find a kiss waiting for them, always.

A rare picture of Rosie Briar dancing. She is framed by the doorway leading to the back veranda. She is wearing a wide-brimmed hat; her mouth widening to the camera with an impulsive, delicious smile. One bare foot is bent foreword, held captive by an audience of wind.

The stillness in Anntell's photograph is poem-like in

nature, the last stanza in a Greek tragedy. Her head is down low, her dark curls dipping into the words on the page of her book. She is in the school library. A stained-glass window to her right, it is patterned into a setting sun.

A small dory is restless upon the rising sea as though waiting for its owner to bring it safely to shore.

Yes, these he would add to the three winning entries he took out west to his collection.

Alfie took three weeks of vacation when he left for New York in his new van. He had plans for when the exhibit was over.

His photography was a big hit. One New York paper headline read: "Self-taught Photographer from the Small Island of Cape Breton-Canada Dazzles New York with his Powerful Images."

He sat in a small café and watched the shapes of New York through the cloudy window. A young couple strolled by and sipped from the same paper bag. An older woman in a long tattered skirt and blouse stopped and waved at him. Her toothless grin gave her face the appearance of a child's ragged doll that had outgrown its owner's love and comfort, discarded with a name nobody even remembers anymore. Alfie waved back to her. He searched the faces of the women who passed by the window. He listened for the sound of their laughter. He finished his coffee and set out on foot on the sidewalks of New York.

Staring. That's what he did for the rest of the day. He went into a posh restaurant and was stopped at the entrance by a rather eccentric maître d' who disapproved of his appearance. His camera bag and running shoes were out of the question for this establishment.

"There's a greasy spoon down the lane," he recommended with a scowl.

Alfie went into old churches where candles on their elaborate stands flamed in all the colours of the rainbow. What had people sought for the price of a dime? Peace, health, faithful husbands, loving wives, missing children. Alfie slipped a dime in the slot and lit a yellow candle, waited until the flame rose an inch or two and set up his camera. When he turned to leave he noticed a young woman in a back pew. Her head bowed, her two hands covering her face. Dark curls, soft and sad, over her slim white hands. Alfie aimed his camera and captured the scene. His heart beat wildly. His hands shook. Could this be possible? Anntell? Here, amongst the candle flames?

And then she lifted her head and Alfie stared into the face of an older woman who appeared startled by him with his camera aimed on her face. He apologized, placed his camera into the bag. For a moment his voice trembled as he told the stranger that he had been looking for someone he knew a while ago. The woman offered up a faint smile and folded back into prayer. Alfie had a feeling she did not understand a word he spoke.

Alfie knew Anntell had left Spain, but she had not contacted her mother to let her know her whereabouts. Could she be in New York? He roamed in and out of bars looking for the one with pictures of Benny Goodman and Louis Armstrong on its walls. He listened for the sound of dead horns at the doors of many others.

One last trip was to the grand library. He stood near the massive stone lions, Patience and Fortitude, at the library entrance. He entered and began his search. No doubt Anntell Briar had, at some time, entered these doors, had stopped and patted Patience and Fortitude, had lost herself among the shelves of books. After a couple of hours of searching and silence, he left.

Rosie had not asked him directly to look for her daughter. She would not interfere with his work schedule. "I don't suppose you'll have much time for sightseeing in New York, Alfie, with all the people you'll have to meet with for one thing or another."

He didn't mention Anntell to her. He knew without having to say anything that she was well aware of his intentions, and aware that if Anntell saw Alfie's photos in the exhibition they might spark a yearning for home.

"I'll have a few spare moments, Rosie. There are a few places I'd like to set my camera on." He smiled at her, knowingly.

He returned to his hotel. Several messages waited for him—requests for photos or interviews. He mulled over the messages like he would a meal of cold eggs. Alfie Clare was not comfortable with this part of his work. He wanted, instead, to comb the streets and museums and bars of New York to search for Anntell. Alfie showered and went to meet Mr. Avery at the Center; they needed to make arrangements for the sale of his work.

A magazine editor, fascinated by the photograph of "The Reader," had requested an interview for lunch the next day. They met at a small elegant café on 5th Avenue. A list of questions ran down the page of his notebook; a grocery list of professional intrusions written in quality penmanship. His edgy, whinny voice was eager to begin. Do you know the beautiful girl in the picture? Is she really from that little island called...? It was the "from" that annoyed Alfie the most.

"Yes, I do know the beautiful girl from the island of Cape Breton."

"Jesus, I could swear she was from New York or Los Angeles."

"You can swear if you like, but she'd still be from Cape Breton."

A short chuckle from the man impressed with the beauty from the little island called....

Alfie was happy to be released from this interview. He refused a lunch. He had someone waiting he said, as he offered his hand to the reporter and thanked him for his interest. He had answered all the questions with a civil tongue. He wished Anntell herself had been present to hear them. He smiled at the thought of it.

When he returned to his hotel, several messages wait for him. He contacted Mr. Avery concerning orders to be filled. There was a new message from a woman named Misty, written in calligraphy on blue paper. She was one of the presenters from somewhere in the mid-west, he recalled, with eight photos of scarecrows in their weather-beaten fashions.

> *Greetings Alfie,*
>
> *How does dinner sound to you? Eight o'clock at The Begotten, a block west of our hotel. We can meet in the lobby at seven thirty if you can make it. They serve great chicken and ribs.*
>
> *Cheers,*
> *Dr. Scarecrow*

He threw the note in the wastebasket. He remembered her from the exhibit's opening, her endless questions about his work, her objections to Scarf being allowed to eat from the hand of a child so frail.

"A scratch from a wild bird can carry many toxic infections."

"That crow was tamer than a lot of people I know. Joseph was in no danger," he informed her in a dark tone.

"One can tell a lot about a person's personality by the photos they take or the things they write. My thesis centred on 'Humpty Dumpty'. I believe the author was fat and awkward. I think the wall he refers to was a bridge he planned to jump off of to end his misery. 'All the king's horses and all the king's men' are his paranoid visions of hospitals and doctors unable to repair his mind. In this exhibit, I've observed five or six people with possible personality disorders, and certainly two with psychotic tendencies. And in no way am I referring to you. But I do sense a latent anger in you, about to burst. It has fermented a long time." She was in her forties, a psychiatrist with a fear of crows who photographed scarecrows in farmers' fields. She believed the scarecrows were almost as essential to the farmer as rain.

He was in no mood for boring lectures that pried for personal information. She reminded him of Bertha Johns; they both chased the dangers they believed they saw in others. He could imagine her and Bertha in front of a mirror holding imaginary conversations with themselves. They would rant until their own images became too disturbed and unhinged, too startled for words at the very moment they recognized themselves.

And he knows this woman will speak, will unload her own baggage and watch slyly to see what he will pick up on. She doesn't listen, but she watches for an opening to get at his weakness. She had mentioned his anger. She was onto something he'd rather keep under wraps. How can he sneak out of the lobby without her noticing him? If he meets her, he can tell her that he is meeting someone else and hurry on.

She was standing at the elevator door when he arrived at the lobby. He stepped out from the elevator and tried to act as politely as the situation would allow.

"Well, I see you received my note! How nice of you to accept."

"So sorry, I have a meeting with a reporter. I'm already late." Alfie brushed past her before she could say anything more, and disappeared into the crowd.

A light mist fell. He felt a nagging headache creeping up the back of his skull. He needed a drink, something with an edge that would pounce on the dialogue in his head. That annoying woman had been right about one thing; his anger with Anntell made him search even more. Alfie checked over his shoulder once or twice, to see if she had followed him. He moved on faster up the street, away from everything, everyone.

Why was he even bothering to search for Anntell? The last he had heard, she was in Spain; that was when Joseph passed away. Yes, she'd left and was probably in Canada again by now. He hadn't heard from her for years, but still he hoped to find some trace of her here in New York. He knew why she ran off, and why she drank. But still her drinking and the length of time she stayed away nagged at him.

He found a bar with a booth that faced the sidewalk.

He threw his jacket in the other seat to give the illusion that he was not alone. He ordered a rum and chaser, the first thing he read on the menu. The waiter named different chasers. Alfie mumbled something or other without looking up.

There was something healing in the large tumbler. Alfie pulled it close to his eye and watched its dark swivel splashing against the ice. He was sitting in a New York bar sipping a dirty wave while a light rain slipped down the windowpane. Cheers to fame, Alfie Clare.

The waiter noticed his empty tumbler and offered to pour him another.

"Just one more will do!" He watched the rain coming down in streams. The lights of the city twinkled in the rain. People kept on the move. Faces looked in at him from under umbrellas. Tears dripped off the edges of buildings.

Alfie paid the bill and left the bar. He was only a few blocks from his hotel as he walked east through the crowds, when he noticed the threadbare woman who had waved in at him earlier that day. Her arms were folded around her body for warmth. He caught up to her and introduced himself. She looked up and smiled as he wrapped his jacket around her shoulders. She was on her way to a shelter she said, as she thanked him for the warmth.

"Are you hungry?"

"Yes, sir, I am."

"Stand under this store front! I'll run in and get you something to eat and a hot drink."

When he returned she had disappeared with his coat. Vanished. He half ran back to the hotel. He sipped slowly on the hot coffee and ate the sandwich.

Alfie felt guilty when he swallowed the last bite. Why had he not taken the woman into the store with him? Walked her to the shelter if that's where she was going. Nighttime in big city rain can produce more than its share of new blades on old skin. They cut deepest at night. He could feel her bones when he wrapped her in his jacket. Alfie rested his head in his hands to keep from shaking. He had not even asked her name. She may have invented one, not remembered that she had been given one once upon a time, that her clothes once had been pretty, her bones strong inside the flesh of a woman.

He folded himself on his bed, wrapped a blanket around himself and slept. His dream woke him in the early hours of the morning.

They were here with him, in his bed, the old tattered doll still wearing his jacket. It is full of New York rain. She is looking for her sandwich, a cold cup of coffee in her hand. Dr. Scarecrow is massaging his temples, a remedy she uses before people go over the edge. She believes he has met with an evil force, and has a special remedy for people from Cape Breton because New

York has a special effect on them. Her fingernails are three inches long and painted red. He feels he is being nailed to the mattress while the discarded doll watches with glee, because he ate her sandwich. And Anntell sits prim and proper against the headboard as naked as the snowflakes that surround her.

"I told mother that you would one day hang us up." She crawls down the bed and orders the other two women to get going. They leave without protest. She pulls him into the wet pool left by the discarded doll.

"Touch me, Alfie!"

He weeps at the sound of her voice. It has not changed after all these years. She is clear and concise. "Touch me!"

"Anntell, Anntell."

"I didn't ask you to speak to me. Touch me, Alfie! I want to feel if I am alive while my brothers bask in their summer graves, so deep not even the moon can toast their bones."

He wants to tell her how much he loves her, but he is forbidden to speak. He is on his back in the pool of his sheet, drowning because of a sandwich. He can taste her skin before she moves down on top of him, an avalanche of snowflakes out of control. His tongue has tasted four or five before her mouth takes over to feed him one at a time. He can feel her cold body melting, breaking up like an ice sculpture because he is splitting her inside out to offer up his heat to her, to let her know he has reached as far as he can go for her. They are both part of the explosion. He can hear someone screaming, himself, weeping as he sits on the floor of his room in his own nakedness, alone and cold as he urinates on the floor of a five-star hotel.

36

HE LEFT NEW YORK two days later, after tying up loose ends and scrubbing the carpet with disinfectant. He had no intentions of leaving that kind of mark on New York. He crossed the border into Canada and made his first stop at Niagara Falls.

The misty rush from the Niagara Falls cleared his head. He watched the *Maid of the Mist* sway like a birdfeeder in the wind filled with newlyweds dressed in colourful hats and jackets. The mighty falls roared, a lion with its silver tongue alerting the captain to keep his distance.

Alfie zoomed in on one young couple. The woman sank her teeth into her lip and gripped the rail like a stevedore holding firmly to a steel pipe. Her companion grinned, amused, his face awash with mist and spray.

Alfie had no idea, while he snapped these photos, why some honeymooners venture into the depth of fear at the beginning of marriage. There had to be a physiological reason for people to introduce such turbulent adventure into their new relationships.

He watched the couples disembark from their cruise. The young terrified woman, he'd captured in his zoom lens, walked a good distance ahead of her husband. He appeared to be trying to explain something to her. She waved him off and stormed into a building. The man stood, still as a windless tree, waiting for her return. Alfie walked off to his van and packed away his camera and tripod. He was weary of being caught up in the lives of damp lovers.

He left Niagara Falls, drove until he reached the Québec border and stayed the night in a small motel. He was anxious to get home—to see how Isla and Rosie were holding up and if they had heard from Anntell. He knew Rosie would tell her that he had been in New York. That part of their life, here in Rocky Point, was on display for thousands of people to admire. They had given Alfie permission to use their images. Isla in her favourite chair beside the hearth, a slow fire teasing some light into her eyes, and Rosie trying a dance step in the open air, and dear Joseph with his hand out to feed Scarf. Anntell had already given permission, years ago, for her own photos to be used wherever he pleased. He never knew if she took his work seriously.

He reached Nova Scotia before sunset and stopped along a route in Truro to shoot a few frames. Several sheep and horses grazed in a green pasture; the setting sun combed through the horses' manes like fire arrows. Alfie set up his tripod and began to capture a series of photos. A couple of the horses looked up and began to walk towards the fence where he stood. A black stallion was in the lead, followed by a chestnut mare. Alfie moved his camera a few feet back from the fence. He watched the stallion's muscles ripple like something under silk hungry for adventure. He tossed his large head back as his black mane poured down his neck like dirty rain. The mare began to gallop until she was nose to nose with the stallion. They both stopped suddenly: the stallion whinnied and punctured the air with a set of sharp uneven yellow teeth; the mare nuzzled her nose between the stallion's teeth. She pulled back and opened her mouth, and they seemed to nibble like children bobbing for apples in the open air.

In the distance Alfie heard the barking of a dog. It appeared in silhouette at the top of the hill and began to run towards him and the bobbing horses. He dismantled his camera from the tripod and packed them in the back seat of his van. A bag with two apples on the front seat caught his eye as he got behind the wheel. Alfie lowered the window and threw them towards the horses. The dog's dark almond eyes watched his every move as though waiting for an intrusion on its territory.

It had stopped barking, but kept its slanted eyes on Alfie as it approached the van with its teeth bared. Its nostrils sputtered venom. A musty slime ran down the corners of its vicious mouth. The dog leapt up to the van's door and peered in the window. A golden collar was secured around its neck with its name tag dangling. "Pyrenees" sniffed at the window of the van and let out a greasy, foul bark. The white dog had a wedge-shaped head and slightly rounded crown. The thick hair on the back of its head gave it a mane-like appearance. Its face had a slight tan colour.

Alfie remembered seeing a picture of this breed of dog in a *National Geographic* magazine. Its breed was also its name. A guardian of animals, Pyrenees did not move until Alfie turned the ignition. The big male dog moved closer to the fence and watched the van drive away. The horses had trotted off up over the hill as Pyrenees stood, as still as a stone, on guard. Alfie went up over a hill and turned around to get a few photos of the dog with its fierce eyes.

Pyrenees was nowhere in sight. The fields were empty, the horses and sheep gone. On the hill, the emptiness of the soft darkening pasture and rolling hills was an avalanche of green grass pouring towards him. He turned and drove away.

Alfie Clare had not thought about Arthur Briar for some time. Most of their encounters had been turbulent, but he respected the sorrow and grief felt by his mother and grandmother at his loss. Poor Arthur, who had the misfortune of inheriting his paternal grandmother's eyes, while his maternal grandmother's colours bled away. Theirs was a family greatly harmed by eyes.

Alfie rolled down the window and sucked in a hard breath. In the silence of the lonely highway, he could recall Arthur Briar's scrambled and frightened voice shouting, "Go-go-go-to hell...white...dog!"

And now he, himself, had encountered an animal much like that Arthur claimed to have seen, and he went looking for the white dog, but for different reasons. Alfie felt a sickening bounce in his gut. He felt Arthur Briar's agony in looking for a dog that didn't exist. But Alfie knew that what he had seen was real, that the mind can keep a watchful eye on fact and fiction and might not reveal the difference until it's too late.

37

ALFIE CLARE BELIEVED that he had come home to go away. Rosie was stable enough to meet the morning with a list of things most people do. She went shopping, had her hair done, kept her doctor's appointments. She inquired about Alfie's trip, and how everything went for him. She let him know that Anntell was back in Québec, living with friends in an old farmhouse.

Isla appeared relaxed and content that all went well for Alfie. She waited until Rosie left the room to speak to him.

"I remember, Alfie, when you often talked about travelling the world with your photography." She tilted her head towards the scent of the man. "Go while your feet can still take you, and your eyes can marvel in the world's beauty. Don't wait for anything that won't wait for you!" He knew her message was about Anntell.

Rosie heard the latter part of the conversation and agreed with her mother.

"She's right, Alfie. You have done more than was necessary for us. It's your turn to set your goals into action. I know you'll be back someday. I've left a token for you at the bank as a gesture of goodwill." He began to protest, but the two women hushed him.

A week later, they said their goodbyes over a roast beef dinner and two bottles of red wine. They were suspended in a moment of bliss and wine when they bid farewell. He felt like a newlywed, trotting off with a row of cans tied behind his car, but without a bride. The gravel screamed under his tires as he drove away.

The morning he left Rocky Point, Alfie Clare went to the cemetery just after dawn to visit Joseph's and Arthur's graves. He wasn't really sure why; he knew it would be stressful to visit. Would he ever return to Rocky Point? He wasn't sure. He had taken a year's leave of absence from the mill, but he kept his rented house at Rosie's insistence. He knew she needed some form of reassurance that he would be back someday.

Arthur's and Joseph's graves were perfectly groomed. Kentucky bluegrass spread as thick as rich velvet. The peak of their marble tombstones rose to meet a morning sun that scorched their names, flashed them out in dual rays. Alfie wondered if there were dialogues people left with the dead. He can't remember what he'd said when he reached Clare's grave. Perhaps silence can offer more than words. There was a small marble plaque on Duncan Briar's grave where none had been before. For some reason, he was pleased to see that Rosie had become strong enough to accept her choice, and to respect Charlie Briar's love for his son.

Duncan William Briar
1890-1967
Lived and died close to the fort

Someone had destroyed him before he destroyed himself. She had always been aware of this. Charlie Briar knew this the day their fort fell, the day that his wife Rowena took it from them. Hate can keep one as close to a person as love can. Charlie needed Rowena's hate to keep loving his son. Duncan needed her love to keep hating her. Poor Arthur was lost in the midst of the rage and pain. All he had to do was stay angry, stay in pain, to free himself, or so he believed. Had he met the lead actors face to face, there might have been a different role for him. Charlie Briar might have kept him safe in the fort.

Alfie walked away slowly from the cemetery. He had a plane to catch, the world to see, and the memory of a girl, he assumed he would never see again, to bear.

38

ALFIE CLARE LOOKED out from the plane window down onto a field of breathing green. He could make out a farmer and young children herding sheep into a pasture as the small plane gained altitude over Rocky Point and they were out of view. Barn doors would open and he knew that the large cattle would sniff the late spring air with an aristocratic tilt of their nostrils before moving out of the barn. They were proud beasts. He was always moved by the way these animals walked from their pen of death without a fight. Farmers did their butchering in spring, chasing the sheep around a fenced-in pen in boots bloodied by slaughter. The lambs protested, making a run for safety; caught in a blizzard of wool and terror, they went silent after the second slice of the blade. Alfie dropped his childhood prayers into each red spill. And when they were hoisted up by the legs to the butchering block, he held tightly to the bowl that would carry their warm livers to Bertha's waiting frying pan. A fresh kill made a tender meal. She'd always insisted that Alfie be present for the kill.

The physical beauty of Rocky Point called for nostalgia, but Alfie Clare was thinking of what lay ahead in his future. He had planned so long for his departure, the gravity of his dream penetrated his skin like an itch. He wanted to see countries that had inspired him as a child, to see faces creased like an accordion by strife, folded by famine and survival. Scarred-faced men tattooed by violence; children, agile as cats, scrounging for scraps of food; and swollen young women who found another way to fill their hunger. He wanted to tread through China, stroll along the great dragon of the wall with its grasslands and deserts serving up solitary splendour. Someday he would visit the Baltic's coastline. Visit Russia's Red Square. Feed his skin to Siberia's bitter bite. He mapped out each entry in dark ink.

His flight from Rocky Point would take him to Halifax, and from there, another would take him to Spain. He felt the weightlessness of a dying man between the clouds, with visions of another world etched on his pupils. He had waited longer than anticipated for this adventure; he had hungered for it for years. Under the blue sky, when the plane rose out of the clouds, the morning sun seared in his eyes.

Alfie turned his gaze from the ball of fire coming through the window. He had taken a morning flight so he wouldn't have to pace around the house for hours. Before he left, he stood looking up at "The Geranium Window," wondering if Joseph were still alive, would he go on this journey. Joseph's eye seemed to follow his every move. A cool sweat ran down Alfie's neck as his hand circled the outline of Joseph's shaded face, a child of shadows.

He had become so frail in the end; Alfie thought of how the two women who loved him so dearly, had to cradle him so delicately. A kiss could leave a bruise. Alfie had worn gloves to carry him around. A dove in a magician's hand is what he was in his arms.

During his flight to Spain it had begun to rain. He looked out the window and watched the raindrops crawl like transparent bugs, their minute bodies drained of all inner parts for the convenience of paying passengers. His mind wandered, recalling the instructions he'd left for the man who took over his position at the mill. He was an older man who had worked at the mill for years. He still carried the scars from Rowena Briar's driving force.

Alfie's mind rested on the first day he met Joseph Briar. From that moment in 1963, he had fit his own life to meet that frail little body of love and pain. Joy and sadness. He had developed from this encounter his moral beliefs. He was not coaxed into these beliefs by any organized religion, by any old wives' tales in Bertha Johns' kitchen. He had cautious sex with nice girls for pleasure. Some of them begged for a second touch, but he declined kindly. He never fell in love with them. He loved Anntell Briar and he had for a long time, but he avoided the dangerous philosophy that escorted her into action. He avoided her sexual invitations, but took them home where he played them out in the dark. He left his sexual life with Anntell Briar between the solitary heat of cotton and flannel.

And now he was headed for Spain and she was somewhere in Québec, translating her sorrow into another language. The unspoiled Mediterranean coastline of Murcia in the south of Spain was a long way from the cool Atlantic coastline of Rocky Point, where drift ice piled up on the sand like dirty broken slabs of concrete. Spain still carried the last of the dust of dictatorship on its knees. But it was being rubbed out to the relief of the gentle, friendly people of Murcia, who greeted this blond stranger with his camera and his broad smile.

Down the coast a small band of three young men, in red vests and dark pants, swayed to their own rhythm. One of the young men caressed a set of small drums, his bronzed hands under the warm sun beating fire with fire. Another strummed a guitar and the third played what appeared to be a wooden flute. In the circle of music, an older couple danced. From under their feet, sand swirled as if the dance required nature to join in. It flew under the woman's flared skirt as she twirled. Her face was flat and her dark eyes radiated small flames. Her mouth lay against her husband's ear. Alfie moved closer to the couple and realized she was singing.

The couple smiled as Alfie snapped their picture. He watched as a parade of a dozen or more small girls, between three and twelve years of age, dressed in long white dresses with orchids in their hair, formed a circle around the couple and held hands. They giggled as they synchronized their steps to the music's increasing tempo. Alfie watched as the children's merry feet stomped up and down, sand collecting between their toes.

A crowd gathered to watch. A young man who noticed the tall stranger pan the crowd with his camera explained the celebration to him in broken English. The couple was celebrating the birth of their first grandson, Manuel the fourth. A gift of spiritual luck from the womb after so many years: fourteen granddaughters, from their four children, and now finally a boy—the infant Manuel, held tightly to the bosom of a yawning young woman, was passed to the father who placed the baby in the circle for his first dance with his grandparents. The child never stirred from sleep. He heard not a chant of joy or the wild call of his name from the chorus of girls surrounding him. He dismissed the taste of their kisses on his handsome face for the sweet surrender of slumber.

Further along the coast, with the faint sound of

music still ringing in his ear, Alfie Clare sat on the edge of a bench. He listened to the low tide chant over the warm sand, then walked back to his hotel along the beach and settled his thirst with a margarita. The Segura River crossed the city from east to west. Night and day, its sorrowful ripples sweetened the air with a never-ending ballad.

The sun seemed to take forever to set. Alfie sat under the shade of a tree near his hotel and watched people walk up and down the white dimpled sand. They were tourists, like him, flashing their foreign apparel and fake tans, and sipping expensive fizz through straws. They believed they were more important under this footing, more secure with the mountains rising like a great fort protecting their safety. They bore the domestic escape of the weary traveller, left everything behind them with each sip: troubled marriages, infidelity, wayward children, boring jobs and endless bills.

Down the beach the small band of music faded as the sun dipped slowly between the seams of lightness and darkness. Physics in slow hues.

39

ALFIE FOUND HIMSELF unexpectedly playing tourist a few days later, wandering the streets of Madrid, when it seemed the hands of Time opened, history in its palms. The warm morning air stifled his steps. He shifted his camera and removed the lens cap as his eye followed a movement in a stone crevice of an ancient church. He set the tripod in place. The white feathers of a tail dipped over the edge of the crevice like a woman's torn glove clinging to a wall. A darker head dipped down, too, to judge the distance they had flown. The pigeons' movements, slow and easy. He smiled; he had not expected to see them in a pair. They usually flew in a flock.

The birds, side by side, looked down towards the cobblestones where he stood. There was no mistaking their elegant breed, the Escampadissa, brought to Spain by the Moors almost a thousand years ago. They turned their heads from side to side, and faced each other in conversation about the man below keeping a curious eye on them. It wasn't likely they would fly from their perch any time soon. They really didn't like to fly, Alfie recalled reading. But he decided to stay as long as it took to get a glimpse of them in flight. They were famous for their flying patterns, with the tips of their wings gracing the sky like waterless rowers. In a group they would fly together, then scatter leaving a broken flurry of feathers below the clouds. And on wing, in a fighter-bomber style, they could dive full speed to trap the peregrine falcon as they were trained to do.

The pigeons tucked themselves further into the crevice as Alfie watched. Light footsteps shuffled across the cobblestones behind him. An old priest in his eighties, dressed in a black robe, hurried up to him. Tufts of hair, thin, white strands on his balding head, appeared to have stubbornly determined to keep growing on what was once a full thick crown of hair. A serene smile trembled between his heavy jowls as his right hand moved in blessing toward the birds.

He turned to Alfie with the quick voice of a much younger man. "Habla Español?"

"I speak only English."

Alfie nodded politely to the priest as he gestured towards the pigeons. "Such magnificent beauty has but one language," the old priest replied in perfect English. "I studied in America."

"That is true of their beauty." Alfie smiled, acknowledging the man's words about the birds.

"You are waiting for them to fly? They know this, and will make you wait. They have been trained by mortal creatures, and like the mortals who have trained them, they have developed a certain pride. The white one is the male, as you can see by his size. He will follow the female. She is the boss, or so I believe."

"You have a great knowledge about these pigeons."

The old man laughed with gusto.

"I have been called a fool by the younger priests for following the pigeons like a child whose gladness has never left his mother's arms."

Alfie smiled at the man's candour.

"I have asked them who has proven their wisdom. Perhaps it is the fool who fills his cup slowly while others believe their cup is already full. They tap my fading crown and tell me they love me." He eyed Alfie directly and winked. "I wipe their spills with a smile."

Alfie looked towards the pigeons firmly perched on their bed of stone. He snapped a few pictures but the birds did not stir.

The old priest called out, "Javier, Pedro." Two young altar boys came running out from behind the church dressed in white robes. They were carrying a long pole with a red flag attached to its end. The priest placed the pole firmly on the ground, then tapped and waved it frantically to catch the birds' attention. The boys watched in wonder as Alfie moved behind his camera and tilted it upward. They were about ten years of age, and seemed to have taken the task assigned to them as a great privilege. They were as solemn as if in church. They stood together, twin sentinels summoned from behind the holy walls where, Alfie assumed, they may have just served on His wooden altar. Their alert eyes darted from the red flag to the pigeons and back again to the young man as still as a statue behind the camera. They seemed to know innately when the scene would unfold and watched for the man's reaction more than the pigeons.

The white pigeon shuffled to flex its wing power; the darker pigeon dipped its crown over the edge and twirled its head from side to side. They stood feather to feather as the red flag swayed. The old priest shifted the pole and pulled back a few feet. The robed boys whispered amongst themselves. Alfie checked his zoom lens. The female turned slowly towards the male and dipped her head over the edge. The male lifted his wings.

The loud church bell rang, sending the young boys off towards the main door of the church, a gust of wind lifting their white robes off the cobblestones. Alfie snapped a quick shot as they disappeared through the big oak doors of the church. The priest bid him a farewell as he trotted off to the side of the stone church, pulling the pole behind him. He fled with his head bowed, a disgruntled fisherman without a catch, alerted by the bell that summoned him into the waters of salvation.

The finale was yet to come. The bell continued to

chime. People thickened in front of the old doors. They glanced over at Alfie and at the pigeons. A quiet laugh rippled towards him. He was sure they were amused by his awe of their famous pigeons.

"Americanos adoraran nada."

An old woman gestured with her hand towards the birds to shoo them away, stop them from soiling her house of worship.

A cloud swallowed the blistering sun. The doors of the church opened and the gathering crowd filed in. The men tipped their hats to the greeter and held them firmly to their sides. Small children kept their eyes on the man whose face was hidden behind the box.

Alfie remained behind his camera. The birds nestled at the edge of the crevice like small children surveying the depth of a cliff. He swiped at the sweat on his brow with one hand. He couldn't remember how long he had been standing on the cobblestones. A burning sensation scaled his calves. He needed something to drink; his tongue smouldered between his teeth. Was he the fire of his own imagination? The pigeons didn't give a damn for a man's vanity or tenacity. He hoped something would happen before the people spilled out of church. Who waits this long for the birds? they would ask each other.

What was he doing with all this? He had a real job in Rocky Point. Anger rippled through his gut and shot upward into his chest. He scanned the crevice once more, and watched as the pigeons moved back a few inches from the edge.

And then it happened. The female spread her wings and rose slowly, rowing in elegant strokes as her partner followed on his white wings. They landed directly on the belfry and bowed their heads.

Back at his hotel Alfie ordered room service: a light dinner and a bottle of wine. He lay on his bed remembering the day's events. The unplanned sighting of the Escampadissa pigeons. He had shot several frames; he had a right to celebrate. He had not expected such an event on this trip.

His thoughts were interrupted by the ringing of his phone. A woman's voice asked for Alfie Clare. "Go ahead, ma'am!" he heard her say.

Rosie Briar's voice. A cold chill shot down his back.

"Hello, Alfie? I'm sorry to interrupt your vacation. All is well here: Mother says hello. You had a call from a curator in Montréal, about a show. I'll give you the name and number to call if you are interested."

Alfie took a deep breath as he scribbled down the name and number. They spoke briefly before he thanked Rosie for relaying the message and put down the phone.

He was alarmed at his response to Rosie's phone call. Although he had given her his whereabouts and number, he had not expected to hear from her. He had assumed a call could only mean an emergency. Her voice had been eager. He sensed the excitement without Rosie even mentioning the possibility that Anntell might turn up if he had a show in Montréal.

Alfie poured himself a glass of wine. He had mixed feelings about going to Montréal to play another game of hide and seek for Anntell. What did he hope to find after seven years? Perhaps he would not even recognize her if they met. He downed his wine quickly and poured himself another glass. He would sleep on the idea of returning home for this exhibition. He had been gone less than three weeks and could feel the pull to move on to something new. Spain had not disappointed him. He would return again.

Alfie sat in a round chair and finished off the bottle of wine. An identical chair stood facing him a few feet away with its bright blue arms hugging the emptiness that filled it. Between the chairs on a low table sat a cast-iron statue of a black bull with the neck of a lamp and shade mounted in the middle of its back. The shade hung over it like an umbrella. Between the bull's ribs, two spears arched out the letter V. A red streak ran down beneath the spears. The bull's sad eyes seemed to stare at the empty chair.

Alfie ordered another bottle of wine. He removed the bull from the table and sat it in the chair. He lifted his glass and toasted his guest with its sad eyes, knowing that this image was captured by manmade rage.

The next morning he made a phone call to Montréal.

40

IT WASN'T WHAT he imagined, standing here before the canvas of Anntell in her red boots, in a place where the rich come to dine on the altar of the nearly unknown. He heard voices behind him critically darting their haute couture opinions.

"Out of control genius, I'd say, with wild virgin impulses for the girl." It was a homely woman behind him who spoke. Gave her champagne glass a tilt and surveyed the bottom of the glass with her eyes crossed.

So he took his turn, non-verbally, unmasked, still damp with his need for Anntell, his love for her, and wrapped his knuckles on the rim of the canvas where she spread her legs, spread her defiance, spread her red boots as deep as she could into a wave to collect a scent, to take with her as he snapped her farewell collection. He honestly believed he was giving her a parting gift back then. Something she needed, she'd said, to remind her of home.

Anntell liked to nest in the shadows, in books like dust, to keep her smiles and sorrows between the lines. Confrontations were easier, they flew off the pages. Her grief disappeared with her, but to where? In Joseph's grave? In Arthur's grave, or even her father's? She needed a deeper space for what unfolded in her life in 1967. Maybe she had sneaked back to Rocky Point unnoticed. But there were no footprints at the gravesite the last time he checked. No red boot prints, unless the Kentucky bluegrass deceived him and tucked them beneath its roots.

He turned and looked directly at the homely critic. She was rather large, in her stripped horizontal sequins and a fringed collar. A tall gentleman grabbed her arm to escort her towards the champagne, but not before she caught Alfie's eye. She knows he knows, he assumed. She had been heard sketching out what she believed was his daring youthful desire on canvas.

She stared into his handsome face with its worry lines sweeping out of the corner of his eyes. He looked older than she'd imagined; a tragic face for one so young. She wanted to question him about the girl, the beautiful and damp secrecy of it all. She looked around. Had he escorted her here? Were they lovers? Suddenly she was more interested in the artist than the art.

Alfie, reading the woman's face, made a quick exit. He watched as several people walked by along the sidewalks. Some of them carried packages and small children into the coming night. Others stopped and looked at the posters laid out in a windowed showcase. Flags of the world waved down to the people along the streets.

From where he stood, he could see clearly the photograph of Joseph's pale hands outstretched towards Scarf. His left hand was slightly elevated, dangly, his vulnerable flesh mapping the bloodlines of his hollowed veins. His right palm slightly opened. The seeds as visible as small flat pebbles, a feast of resistance for the crow.

How often had he looked at these photographs and had some new nugget tap into him deeply? He looked towards the street again. Many people were filing into the museum. Some of them recognized him from his photo and greeted him with a nod. He wanted to leave, felt out of place. Caught in between strangers' tastes and distastes. What did he really care about the assumptions of others?

Rosie had not mentioned her daughter when last they spoke. Perhaps Anntell was not communicating again; silence has no address. He scanned the faces of the crowd, gazed into every one looking for a familiar trait. He would know her eyes anywhere. She must have seen something in the papers about the show. Alfie took a deep breath; let thin air settle in his lungs.

Someone requested an interview. What more could he say about his art? About his passion for suspending women in eternal youth, his beloved Anntell and Clare? His desire to keeps birds in perpetual flight? But most of all, what could he say about his need to keep Joseph in view? How what is erased floats by in front of him, rising from wooden planks: Joseph, breaking through his shell, coming towards the noise between Alfie's teeth, whistling through the geraniums. Perhaps he imagined birdsong falling with the rain and he let his small drum go cold and came to listen. His broken body shivered and Alfie's heart tumbled in his chest. The reality of Arthur's wild story staggering towards him.

Alfie Clare caught an image of himself in a dim mirror on his way back to his exhibition. He stepped back, zoomed in. Was it the hurt or harried contours of his face that frightened him? His hair was still a youthful blond, cut shorter than usual. Easier for travel to shed a few curls. His tan from Spain had bronzed his six-foot-two frame. He had gained extra pounds, drank himself into a thirty-six inch waist. Straight even teeth collided with the rim of the wine glass he held, shaved his tongue on the edge of the glass. A blade in his sour mouth.

Alfie looked at his watch—it was just past seven; he wished to God it was closer to nine p.m., when the gallery closed. There was still enough light left of summer to keep people hanging around a large city.

He envied artists who preferred the dark. Mozart

did his best composing at night, without interruptions. He scribbled his scores on the back of night's cold hardships, only releasing them to paper in the light of day. Alfie worked in reverse. He preferred the light, needed it. At night, what he captured by day, and what he lost, came at him. Shivering ghosts.

He remembered Rosie Briar telling him how she saw her children much clearer when their heads were full of sleep. Their faces opened up like a flower blooming when she approached their beds.

Anntell was like the wild rose. Prickly to the touch, yet those layered petals matched her personality. She never cared which way the wind blew, but her beauty was dangerous in a storm. She was speaking of the litter that lingers with grief. It was always in the way, no matter how hard she tried to have it hauled away. It clung to her sentences. She placed her name in the most obscure places, the weather, in the depth of snow, the colour of mittens, the shape of a cat's paw.

And Arthur was her tiger lily, spotted and hard rooted. They'd grown wildly in her mother's garden. He'd ask her night after night to tell him the legend of the tiger lily in his grandma's garden. Rosie hadn't bothered with gardens at the Briar house. It was the kind of land that would betray beauty.

Her face had grown cloudy. She pushed the words upward from deep within her. She wanted someone to understand her son between his dark moods, his sullen behaviour, between his need for attention and recognition, his handsomeness and ugliness; how desperately he wanted to be his own person. Tiger lilies prefer the wild, turn ditches into superior gardens tended by an unseen gardener. Rosie's voice heightened and pushed out a smile.

"My mother first told me the story of the tiger lily. A hermit pulled an arrow from a wounded tiger. The tiger asked the man to befriend him even in death. The man agreed. When the tiger died his body turned into a tiger lily. Eventually the hermit drowned and his body was never found. This is why the tiger lily spread everywhere. It was the tiger searching for his friend who saved him from the arrow. Arthur loved this old legend.

"But Joseph? My little one was drawn to geraniums even as a baby. He collected gladness from behind those plants. They needed to be loved and nurtured as he did. The plants on his window ledge always grew hale and hardy. I'll never know what he saw or heard behind his little jungle."

She was proud of her youngest child's gladness. The sun rippled off her soft skin. Her eyes blinked at the sudden warmth that caught up to her. She seemed to be listening for something coming from a distance. Everything is in her memory now. Moving forward. Collecting words to reconstruct her children's faces, their personalities, their moods, and the tender flesh she reaches out to touch when a song cries out their names.

The quiet, softly lit gallery seems almost pastoral. A young, dark-haired woman from a local paper approaches Alfie and asks if they can find a corner away from the thickening crowd so she can put a few questions to him. She is brisk and direct.

"I can't stand elbow conversations. This way I get my own answers to my own questions. N'est-ce pas?"

He follows behind her without commenting on her theory. They find two chairs and face each other on a slight angle. She takes one stern look around the gallery at the crowd, and goes over her list of questions, her pen placed between her teeth.

"I didn't know you from a hole in the ground until my editor gave me your bio and photo," she begins without lifting her head.

Alfie smiles.

"I came to the gallery before the show opened to see your work. I spent a great deal of time studying it and thinking about your themes." She states firmly like a teacher going over a student's test paper.

Alfie studies the young woman's face.

"Could it be said, Mr. Clare, that you have a fetish for feet? The girl tanning in a bikini and the young girls in Spain dancing up a storm in the sand. And then there's the barefooted infant placed in the circle."

"I would hope to have a passion for beauty," he interrupts her.

She inhales deeply and sighs.

Alfie looks directly into her eyes. They are small and set far apart; her forehead protrudes slightly like an awning over a window to provide shade. The left side of her face is heavily masked in make-up to hide a birthmark. Small lines run from under her nose down toward her lip. She has, no doubt, had a few surgeries to correct her cleft palate. Yet her long dark hair is full of joy, and bounces gracefully over her thin shoulders. He realizes why she wanted to find a quiet corner, why she had come to the gallery before the crowd. She prefers to be invisible.

"People like you don't photograph the ugly like me."

He is troubled by her blunt challenge to him.

"I would be happy to photograph you. I don't see what you think you see."

He realizes his answer is lame. It is what she has already heard. She had perhaps expected something original from him. If you care to create beauty, you should be able to explain it as well.

Her face is expressionless. Blank. That canvas of flesh that suspends itself between belief and disbelief. Here is a stranger explaining ugliness to him in a corner she has boxed him in. Chastising him for presenting beauty and ignoring the ugliness she is pointing out in herself.

He begins to explain his photograph of the geraniums to the woman. A loud skirmish interrupts the conversation near the front entrance. Alfie looks towards the door, where several security guards form a barrier. An angry voice slips in past the guards. Alfie hears two of the guards conversing to one another.

"She's been here before; comes in from that drunk-tank a few blocks away. A tough little bitch, but she's mellowed in the last few months. Been asking lately about the artist, Alfie Clare."

Another guard speaks in French with the girl. She is quick to respond. A bilingual retort followed by a short pause, and then she is speaking English again. Her voice is split, uneven, scrubbed raw.

She has the upper hand on these guards even now. Her insistence is too heavy in the face of their light imaginations. She demands to see the exhibit. It is hers to see, she insists. Most of the photographs are of her and her family. A roar of laughter shuffles through the crowd.

She is fighting the ugliness in their laughter, their ignorance, reaching out for what is left of her own flesh and blood beauty, what is left of it, a few feet from her—hanging on the walls under lights as soft as the little moons that faded at dawn through her bedroom window in Rocky Point.

"La folle," someone calls out. "Phone the police!"

Alfie wants to stop what is about to happen. His

mouth is dry and the thickness of his tongue makes him appear intoxicated, too. He hates the feeling that stops him from using his natural voice. He knows who the guards have cordoned off. He wants to reach out to her. Touch her and let her know he is here to protect her.

There is a scramble of French and English dialogue again, but her voice comes out loud and clear. She is not speaking French but her own Rocky Point English as she aims her words directly into the crowd like a dart.

"Fuck-Off! Fuck-off, you fools. You don't have a clue about me or this art!"

Alfie can see the hem of her blue dress as she frees herself from the guards and rushes towards the front entrance with a shoe in her hand. He moves quickly behind her, calling out her name. She is out on the sidewalk in her bare feet. Her blue, high-heeled shoes scattered along the walkway. He calls out her name, but she doesn't respond.

She makes her way down the sidewalk towards the corner of Dorchester and Mansfield Street, past the Queen Elizabeth Hotel where Alfie is staying. She is running east on Belmont Street towards the Central Train Station. It is here that he loses sight of her when she enters the station. A blue blur against a background of shrieks and whistles, people and shops. Is this his last chance to see her, to speak to her?

He scrambles through a crowd of pent-up teenagers.

They awkwardly shove off as he rushes towards them.

"What's the rush, man?"

Alfie mumbles a weak apology to the teenagers as he searches the crowd.

"I'm looking for a woman," he pleads.

"Aren't we all!" they chuckle as they call out to him. "But we're not as desperate as you!"

He passes an elegant restaurant: a few couples, dressed for a night on the town, toast each other with the click of their glasses, a sexual ring for round one. They are oblivious to the young man, his adrenaline on fire in this underground city.

Alfie sees a sign indicating tracks and makes his way quickly to the front of the line. Someone asks for his ticket and he blindly hands him a twenty. He is down in a subway station, elbow to elbow with tired and hurried passengers. Anntell? Where is she? He can't see her anywhere, takes the escalator three steps at a time. How in the hell did he lose sight of her? She was at his fingertips. Why didn't he try harder to break through the crowd?

He hears the shrill sound of police whistles. His body stiffens, his bones locking like an iron gate. Several policemen rush by followed by a stretcher and paramedics. People split a path for them to pass. They make their way towards the CNR passenger train section. His tongue is a knot trying to untie itself. A choking feeling pulls at his throat. Tightens. Releases enough air for him to call out to her.

"Anntell? Anntell, answer me!"

People hurry past him as they pretend not to notice the young man talking to himself. A few couples pick up their children as they walk by. A crowd gathers at the end of the train line. Someone has wrapped a blanket over a body on the platform. A woman is shrieking out a name. She is asking what happened to her husband. Two of the policemen escort her through a side door.

Alfie follows a long corridor. He has no direction in mind, and no idea of how he made it this deep underground. The smell of grease and oil makes his stomach churn. He comes to another opening. It is almost abandoned except for a few stragglers hunched over on wooden benches in a waiting room. A battered old suitcase, covered in stickers, lies at a young man's feet. His guitar case that leans against the back wall; an "I've Been Everywhere" sticker echoes the old Hank Snow tune.

"You heading back east?" The young man is looking up at Alfie with doleful eyes. "I can't wait to get home," he continues. "I had enough of this city." His life's defeat in one sentence.

Alfie nods his head and keeps searching. He can't waste any time. He leaves the room and keeps walking. There are several tracks as he looks down into the pit. A train snails its way towards a tunnel, "OUT of

SERVICE" flashing on the front where the destination is always posted.

His eyes hurt. He should have had her paged. Let her know that they are close to finding each other. He keeps walking along the platform as workers descend and mingle in small groups. They notice him but do not question him. He begins to replay the conversations at the gallery. He'd heard one of the guards mention a program for people with drinking problems. She was trying to help herself. She had gone for help.

He is frustrated even more by the fact that he doesn't know where he is or how he even made his way down here without being questioned. And if he informs the police it could spell trouble for Anntell. A barefoot woman in a train station shouldn't be hard to find and detain. The gallery had probably already called the police. Their first stop would have been the detox centre where she was living. They had more than likely given up when she was not there. Wrote her off as a runaway delusional who believes she'd found herself a family hanging on a gallery wall.

Alfie continues down a passageway. Was he to blame for Anntell's peril? Had he been able to keep her there in the gallery he would have cleared things, made them right for her by acknowledging her identity. The guards had formed a chain and let nobody through. He had caught the eye of the reporter as he rushed towards Anntell, saw the realization of the truth dawning on her face—this irate woman was the girl in the red boots.

He rounds a corner and is face to face with another pit of tracks. Posted on a signboard for 17:21, destinations blinking in cool block letters. In less than an hour, the platform will be filled with passengers boarding for the Maritimes, its final destination.

Alfie Clare slides his back down the tiled wall and shuffles his feet out in front of him. He is not just weary, he is despondent. He removes his shoes and feels a cool draft play between his toes. He has run out of corners and passages. A man leaning on a platform with nowhere to go. He closes his eyes, buries his thoughts in the dark. He will have to tell Rosie that she'd slipped away again. Sober and determined that someone had failed her again. That she had appeared at the gallery and fought to be let in.

And Rosie Briar will remember her daughter's words ever so clearly.

"He'll hang us up one of these days."

Alfie opens his eyes to a rumble he hears in the distance. It sounds like thunder but he is too far underground to hear thunder. He sees a blur across the tracks, a blue motion. And she is there, sitting at the edge of the tracks, her head between her knees. A dark mass of hair hides her hands. Her bare feet tilt slightly over the edge like a child inching her way, little by little, into deep water.

This time his voice is bursting his lungs. He can feel a sharp pain when he calls out her name.

"Anntell, pull back; I can hear a train approaching!"

She has not moved. He is not sure she heard him call out. He grabs the edge of the platform and slides down into the pit, tripping over the track in his bare feet. He moves slowly towards her. He can feel a chill breeze tearing up his shirt. The rumble wheezes closer. Something is hooking into his shirt and Alfie rips open the front to free himself. He cannot feel his feet now; he is moving in animated motion.

"Anntell, pull away from the edge!"

He is getting closer to her, but she has not looked up. She appears to be suspended in her own cold isolation. To move may be painful. He knows this type of pain; it locks you in for the melt. He has to get her attention. Alfie reaches out, but he's not close enough to grab her foot. He takes one more step, but stumbles again. His jaw crashes against the steel rail.

Searing lights are coming towards him. There is a sputtering of brakes; a deep angry grind and a violent whistle that slices into his brain. He cannot hear the sound of his own voice screaming at Anntell. Alfie looks towards the orange steel bulk that is still moving. An iron grill on its front resembles a handlebar moustache.

They are going to be crushed to death by a god-damned mustache.

He makes one more leap towards Anntell. He can feel part of her ankle. She looks up slowly and raises her hands frantically towards him. A voice is screaming from inside the train.

"There are cleaner ways to die, you goddamned idiot."

He can feel nothing now. Suspended in weightlessness, his mind has ejected everything. Perhaps this is a prerequisite for departure, to leave all your baggage behind. She will be with him. He has found her in time for death.

41

AND THIS IS how the passers-by would have seen the couple on the train platform. Huddled together like the Raggedy Anne and Andy of Central Station. Two torn and abandoned dolls. The brilliant artist with his knuckles exposing raw bones; the beautiful woman exposing her wounded foot. The other was spared.

His tattered shirt, stained with grease and blood, clinging in shreds to his bare back. On his grey face, the colour of dried cement, the look of violent euphoria cracking open between its bloody seams. He had taken on a train and won.

His hands slip down her dress, light cotton shredding gauze under his nails. Her feet bare. Her left foot is bruising up like a wild storm. She pays it little attention. They lean against the wall of Central Station. Its cool tiles bleed relief into their young bones. She holds out his hands for inspection and brings them to her mouth to kiss the broken flesh. Alfie's blood the taste of sweet warm cider.

How else would Anntell have wished for death? He can see her face clearly now. She is looking back at him through strands of black hair. Her eyes clear, grown up, sober, older than they should be, starving for someone or something familiar. Alfie knows this look—Rosie Briar's eyes have long held it. They are a family whose eyes give way to misery.

They hear the hissing of an oncoming train. It sweeps past them in a great silver streak. They inhale the wind it lends them. A flutter of debris falls close to Alfie's side. Someone's one-way ticket; a smudge of grime smearing the final destination: Sydney, Nova Scotia.

Anntell is trembling in his arms. He pulls her closer into him to soothe the tremors of shock shooting up from her slim body. She has not said a word since she pulled him up off the tracks. He wants to hear her voice, but he will wait. He will wait as he did in Spain to see the pigeons soar.

They put her on the first stretcher that arrives. She is in and out of consciousness. Alfie insists he must go along with her. He cannot leave her alone. She is lucid when they reach the emergency ward. She glances at her bare feet unravelling from the sheet as they check out her wounds. Her left foot, turning black now, like a Saturday night punch. She struggles to get out of the sheet, fighting her way free. He wishes he had his camera with him as he studies her foot. They will laugh at these times in the future. He is sure of this.

"Alfie, I am clean, finally clean. I was on my way..."
Coming from under the sheet, her voice has the softness of truth.

He reaches over and whispers her name before she drifts off into a clean, deep sleep.

ACKNOWLEDGMENTS

Many thanks to the fine tuning of my manuscript by editors James Langer and Marnie Parsons, for their skills in the art of fiction. And to Donna D'Amour, my dear friend and fellow author, for her copyediting and helpful suggestions along the way.

Beatrice MacNeil is the bestselling author of *The Moonlight Skater*, *Butterflies Dance in the Dark*, *Where White Horses Gallop*, and *Keeper of Tides*. She has won the Dartmouth Book Award on three occasions and the Tic Butler Award for outstanding contribution to Cape Breton writing and culture. She lives in Cape Breton, NS.